SWEPT AWAY

A Honeymoon Novella

Squeaky Clean Mysteries, Book 11.5

By Christy Barritt

CHRISTY BARRITT

SWEPT AWAY: A Novel

Copyright 2016 by Christy Barritt

Published by River Heights Press

Cover design by The Killion Group

SWEPT AWAY

CHAPTER 1

"I had to search far and wide, Gabby, but I finally found the perfect location," Riley said.

Something close to pure delight oozed through my chest at the sound of Riley's—no, make that *my husband's*—voice. I couldn't wait to enjoy seven full days of alone time with him.

"The perfect location, huh?" I said. "I hate to say this, because I know you worked hard on our honeymoon plans, but anywhere with you is perfect."

"I feel the same," he said.

Riley squeezed my hand as we cruised down the road in a rental car. I had no idea exactly where we were since a blindfold covered my eyes, but I was okay with that. We'd gotten married quickly two weeks ago at the end of September, and I'd figured we might get around to honeymooning next summer at the earliest, due to both of our crazy schedules.

"You have no idea how challenging this was," Riley said. "But I knew an island far off the coast was out, especially after the whole Cemetery Island fiasco."

"True." A secluded island and being cut off from the outside world had scarred me for life.

"I knew a resort was out of the question after the whole Healthy Springs episode."

"True again." A missing woman in a highbrow resort had made me never want to go to another one.

"A mountain cabin just didn't seem appropriate after Mythical Falls."

"I can't argue with that." A creepy abandoned theme park and Bigfoot sightings were enough to give anyone nightmares.

Riley pulled the car to a stop and cut the engine. "So, I pulled a few strings, and here we are."

Anticipation sizzled through me. I couldn't wait to see what he had planned. Something about the surprise of it all made me feel like a detective at her first crime scene.

"Can I take my blindfold off yet?" My fingers reached for the soft cotton hankie.

We'd gotten off the plane in Florida, so I knew which state I was in, at least. But as soon as we'd rented a car, my eyes had been covered, and I'd placed myself in Riley's capable hands. As the blare of the AC faded and silence filled the air around me, another ripple of excitement rushed through me.

It had been ages since I had a real, genuine vacation. Come to think of it . . . had I ever had a real vacation? I couldn't remember. I'd traveled, but it was always for work or purposes other than relaxation and fun.

"Stay right there. I'm coming around to get you."

Riley's door opened, and a whiff of heavy, salty air drifted into the car along with the sound of seagulls.

I'd been trying to use my detecting skills to figure out where we were. Based on the sun's location, I figured we were headed west. Based on traffic, which had started out as heavy but gradually eased, I figured we were outside the city limits. Based on the smell and the sounds, I'd guess we were on the Gulf Coast somewhere.

My door opened, and Riley clutched my arm, gently easing me from the sedan. Once I stood on solid concrete beneath my feet, I expected him to take the handkerchief from my eyes.

He didn't.

Instead, he tugged me across the ground until my feet hit something soft. Sand, probably. The scent of salty air hit me even stronger. Since I lived near Virginia Beach, the smell made me feel right at home.

"You ready?" Riley stood behind me, his touch making my skin come alive.

He sounded so cute in his excitement. All of this just reaffirmed how much I loved this man. I couldn't wait to spend the rest of my life with him.

"I'm ready," I told him, not bothering to hide my smile.

He carefully untied the cloth, and my eyelids fluttered open, adjusting to their newfound freedom. I sucked in a deep breath at the sight before me.

The sun sank in front of us, as if it had waited for us to arrive before putting on its show. Pink and purple smeared across the sky. The Gulf waters, though late in the day and absent of any bright sunshine, were still crystal blue and clear. The sandy beach looked white and pristine.

It was one of the most beautiful sunsets I'd ever seen.

"Do you like it?" Riley asked, his breath warm on my ear as his arms circled my waist.

"I love it." I turned and wrapped my arms around his neck. We both pivoted so we could still see the spectacular display on the horizon. "I grew up near the beach, so I thought I'd seen and experienced it all."

"There's something different about the waters down here. And watching the sunset on the Gulf . . . it's amazing."

"I agree." I glanced behind us and spotted a three-story house with an entire wall of windows facing the water.

The place looked grand and fancy with multiple porches and decks and even a little gazebo, all trimmed in a neat white. The building itself was covered in a rich coral-colored siding. Colorful Adirondack chairs rested outside, beckoning people to sit and enjoy the scenery. The bottom level appeared to be mostly pilings that set the residence up high in case floodwaters came.

The nearest house looked to be a good three hundred feet away, and it was a monster, surrounded on two sides by water as the land jutted out into a point. We seemed to be in an exclusive residential area, but just a little farther down the shoreline I spotted a marina and a small town.

"Where are we exactly?"

"Crystal Key," he said. "It's not actually a part of the Florida Keys. We're still a couple of hours away. But we're on an island off the west coast of Florida, about an hour south of Clearwater."

"I love it."

Riley looked back at the house. "A friend owns this place and offered to let us use it. I couldn't come up with a single reason not to. It fit all my criteria."

I turned to face him again, not really wanting to look at the house or the sunset anymore. Just Riley. My husband. The man I loved. Heartache had pulled us closer and pushed us apart only to eventually solidify our relationship for good.

My heart quickened at the sight of him. He looked so handsome. Since he'd taken up mixed martial arts last year, his slim, tall frame had turned into all lean muscle. He had dark hair and was usually clean shaven, but whenever he had the chance lately he let a five o'clock shadow form. I actually liked the look. His blue eyes were kind and wise, he had an easy smile, and he was a great listener. In other words, he was everything I'd ever wanted.

"I'm glad you picked this place. It's nice."

His eyes twinkled. "I planned this carefully, you know. We're staying by ourselves, so there's no one else around to distract us. There's no mysterious history haunting the place. The crime rate is practically nonexistent. There have never been any murders—yes, I researched it. The biggest excitement around here was when the grill didn't work during a local fish fry about a month ago. I think we should actually be able to enjoy our honeymoon like two normal people."

I raised an eyebrow. "Whoever said we were normal?"

"True that." He leaned toward me and planted a soft kiss on my lips. "You ready to grab our bags and get inside?"

My heart fluttered again. I hoped that feeling never left me when I looked at Riley. "Let's go."

We'd only taken one step toward the door when a sound caught my ear, and I stopped.

It sounded like an army was rolling into town somewhere in the not-so-distant distance. Riley's grip at my waist tightened, as he seemed to anticipate the worst also. We both sensed something on the horizon was threatening our plan for peace and solitude.

A convoy of probably ten vehicles—all kinds, from SUVs to vans to limos—appeared on the road and stopped at the massive house beside ours. All at once, people began pouring from the vehicles. Mostly girls. Giggling. In bathing suits. *Tiny* bathing suits.

I was tempted to cover Riley's eyes—the last thing I wanted was Ms. America swimsuit models lounging beside me on my honeymoon. But I trusted Riley. He wasn't the type to gawk.

Three men with cameras also appeared, along with a couple of people with clipboards and other people hauling out equipment of some sort.

The girls continued to giggle as they hurried toward the beach. I halfway expected to see Annette Funicello and Frankie Avalon appear singing "Beach Party."

Riley and I glanced at each other, and neither of us had to say a word.

This had not been on Riley's agenda. *They* had not been a part of the plan.

One last car pulled up. A limo constructed from a Hummer, at that.

A man stepped from the back wearing a white suit and sunglasses. He had curly dark hair and an air of charisma about him.

As soon as he cleared the vehicle, the women went crazy. "Ricky! It's Ricky! Hi, Ricky! Over here, Ricky!"

He grinned a Hollywood type of grin and sauntered toward them. As soon as he reached the sand, the women surrounded him and began fawning over the man. He didn't seem to mind.

All I could think of was "harem."

Maybe, if I blinked, all of these people would be gone, and Riley and I could have our nice, quiet honeymoon. We deserved that much, didn't we?

One of the men toting a clipboard sauntered across the grassy sand toward us. He had a sun-kissed face with thinning, light-brown hair, and a smile that screamed "salesman." His clothing was an updated throwback to the old show *Miami Vice*: a light-colored sports coat, a pink T-shirt, and aviator sunglasses.

"Wally Walker." He extended his hand, a businesslike smile on his face. For some reason, the man looked slightly familiar.

Riley seemed to hesitate before returning the gesture. "Riley Thomas. This is my wife, Gabby."

"Pleasure to meet you both." He nodded toward the house behind us. "You staying here?"

"Yes, we are," Riley said. "On our honeymoon."

The man grunted. "Interesting. We were told no one would be here."

"Who told you that?" Riley asked.

"The owner. We called him about a month ago when we were scouting out locations."

"Well, this was last minute," Riley said. "He must have forgotten."

The man grunted again. "We can work around you two."

"Work around us?" I asked, totally confused or maybe just in denial. I gripped Riley's arm more tightly as anticipation of bad news built inside me.

"Sorry. I'm the host and one of the producers for *Looking for Love*. You heard of us?" Before I could answer, he continued. "We're a reality show. Ten women. One rich, handsome man looking for a soul mate . . . or a trophy wife. Nobody really knows nowadays." He let out a canned laugh. "Anyway, we'll be filming here on Crystal Key this week."

Wasn't that just perfect? Like I'd thought earlier: harem. That had always been my opinion of those reality dating shows.

I had watched the show a couple of times. There was always a handsome bachelor who was called Mr. Eligible, or, during the seasons when a female was the lead, she was called Ms. Eligible. The show's star went on exotic dates with contestants, mostly after they won crazy competitions where time alone with Eligible was the prize. The contestants were given dance cards that promised them a place on the show for another week.

"What's that mean for us?" Riley asked, pulling me closer in a silent apology. He didn't have to say it. I knew him well enough to read the gesture.

Wally thrust a clipboard toward us. "Would you mind signing these release forms?"

"Why would we need release forms?" I asked, staring at the very detailed paper in front of me. The fine print was overwhelming, to say the least.

"Just in case we're filming and we catch you on camera. We hope that doesn't happen." He leaned closer. "Like, we *really* hope that doesn't happen. Like, if you could try to stay out of our way, that would be the best."

We both stared at him until he shrugged without a mere hint of shame.

"But, just in case, we want to cover all our bases. Lawsuits are not our friend." He let out a long, fake laugh.

"I only charge ten thousand for appearances on camera," I said, keeping my expression neutral. "Can we put that in the contract?"

The man's eyes widened, and he let out another forced laugh. "Wh . . . what?"

I smiled, big and broad. "Just kidding."

It's actually twenty thousand. I mentally laughed at myself and then patted my own back for not saying it out loud.

His laugh deepened. "You're a funny one. You two looking for limelight? I have some other shows I'm producing, and we're always looking for camera-worthy faces—"

"No," Riley and I both said at the same time.

Wally raised his hand. "That was loud and clear. Now, about these forms . . . ?"

"I'll read them over," Riley said. He was an attorney, so at least he knew what to look for.

"Fine. I'll come back tomorrow morning to pick them up. How's that sound?"

"Not too early," I pleaded with him

"Sure, sure." He took a step away. "Oh, and by the way—I'm sorry."

"Sorry for what?"

He shrugged apologetically. "You'll see."

***

I was sleeping in Riley's arms, dreaming about paradise and happy-ever-after when a sound jerked me from my happy slumber.

Thump, thump, thump.

I tried to ignore it and enjoy this moment I'd been dreaming about for so long—being married to Riley. Being here. Being with him.

Maybe I'd been hearing things. Maybe it was a dream. After all, it was the middle of the night in the town without crime.

Thump, thump, thump.

The sound became more urgent, and I couldn't pretend I was hearing things.

Somebody was pounding on the door to our beach house.

If I had to guess, this had something to do with the reality show next door. The ladies over there had partied hard until two in the morning, with music blaring and loud, loud talking. It had sounded like festivity central.

What could be happening now to pull me out of my slumber?

Option one: Someone didn't get a dance card.

Option two: Someone had a clothing malfunction.

Option three: Someone found out Ricky the Gigolo was dating someone else.

Riley stirred beside me. "What is that . . . ?"

"I'm not sure. But I guess we should go check it out."

He kissed my shoulder. "Do we have to?"

Just then, someone screamed in the distance, "Please. Help me!"

Riley and I threw off the soft down comforter and

jumped out of bed. I grabbed a robe and quickly tied it around me as Riley and I rushed toward the sound. The scream sounded like more than *Looking for Love* gone bad. Someone sounded scared.

I glanced at the bedside clock. Four a.m.

At the front door, Riley pushed me behind him and finished pulling on his T-shirt. As he jerked the door open, tension crackled in the air. The ocean breeze drifted inside, deceitfully peaceful and balmy.

A woman stood there. Mascara streaked her cheeks, and sand clung to her itsy-bitsy black dress.

"You've got to help me. Please!" She tumbled inside and fell against Riley, heaving in deep gulps of air.

"What's wrong?" Riley grasped her arms. If he let go, she'd surely slip to the ground.

She looked up at us, her eyes wide and tear-rimmed. "They took her."

I touched her arm, concern ricocheting through me. Something had happened to traumatize the woman. Something bad.

I glanced outside beyond the woman and saw nothing but a dark beach. Nothing else was discernable through the blackness of the night. Just what was hiding out there in the nighttime?

"Took who?" Riley asked the woman.

"Vivian." She sobbed again. "We were walking down on the beach when these men pulled up in a boat. They jumped out, grabbed Vivian, and took off. One of them started to come after me, but I got away. This was the first house I found. Please, you've got to do something!"

Riley and I exchanged a glance.

So much for a peaceful honeymoon.

SWEPT AWAY

CHAPTER 2

Riley darted outside to check out things himself—a role I desperately wanted to take, but I restrained myself. Instead, I called 911 and started a pot of coffee— thankfully the owner had left some supplies—and I found a blanket to drape over the woman's shoulders.

As I poured some coffee, I glanced over at her. She'd told me as I led her to the couch a few moments earlier that her name was Joey Hedges and she was originally from Wisconsin. She was a pretty woman—it was a prerequisite for being on these shows. She had flawless olive skin and lovely, dark hair that had just the right amount of gloss. A certain Midwest, girl-next-door charm emanated from her.

I walked toward her, noting how she gripped the soft, blue blanket around her shoulders. Her back was hunched; she clenched a rumpled tissue in her hands; and red rimmed her dark eyes. She was here with me, yet she wasn't. Her mind looked a million miles away.

I quickly glanced out the windows before I reached

her side. When would Riley be back? Had he found anything outside? Was he okay?

Please, Lord.

Just then, the door flew open, bringing with it the briny smell from outside. Riley stepped inside, stomping the sand from his feet. His shirt was already damp with humidity and salty air.

But he was okay. Thank goodness, he was okay.

"Anything?" I paused mid-step, my curiosity skyrocketing.

He shook his head, gently closing—and locking—the door behind him. "Nothing. Whoever was out there is now long gone. It's hard to see anything else because of the dark, but I have a feeling the tide will wash away any evidence like footprints that may have been left."

I tried to ignore it, but something started to sizzle in my blood at his words. A missing woman. An exotic locale. An intriguing mystery.

But I was on my honeymoon, I reminded myself. This was the perfect time to just focus on my relationship with Riley. To stay out of trouble. To mind my own business in the midst of the chaos around me.

But it was as if trouble called to me like a seagull crying out for the seashore. However, I was determined to learn the fine art of ignoring my crime-solving instincts, especially when other priorities beckoned. Like my marriage.

"The police are on their way," I told Joey, who still looked forlorn on the couch as I handed her some coffee.

She dragged her gaze toward me. "Thank you."

"Do you want us to call the guys from the show?" Riley walked toward her, his voice low and compassionate.

She shook her head. "No. I want the police to handle this. I'm tired of the way Alastair handles things."

"Alastair?" Riley questioned as he lowered himself into the white leather recliner across from her.

She frowned. Or was she pouting? "He's the executive producer. He'll do anything for ratings. He'll probably even try to use this to make a few bucks. That's the kind of person he is."

"What happened out there exactly?" I crossed my legs and gripped my own cup of coffee. I tried to keep my voice light, knowing that my curiosity would only seem morbid and insensitive.

"Vivian wanted to talk to me," she started, sniffling and gingerly wiping under her eyes with a French-tipped finger. "We'd had a lot of disagreements since the show started."

"You didn't know her before the show, right?" I tried to keep her talking and calm. Okay, okay—I also wanted more information and background. But *not* because I was investigating

She nodded, bouncing her head up and down at just the right cadence to be Emmy worthy. "That's right. I didn't know anyone. But, right from the start, neither of us liked each other."

"Why was that?" Riley leaned forward, his elbows perched on his knees, as he listened carefully to her story.

Joey sniffled again. "We were both front runners, so there was a bit of competition between the two of us."

I wondered just how far this competition went. Enough to make Joey a suspect? Though she was obviously upset, her archenemy had essentially just been eliminated. With no witnesses around, it was Joey's word against . . . no one's.

Not that I was speculating or forming theories.

"Are you allowed to leave the house while filming is going on?" Riley asked. "That's not against any of the rules?"

His question seemed strange to me, especially since there were so many other things he could be asking. Why wouldn't she be able to leave? It wasn't like she was a prisoner there. Besides, I hadn't realized he knew so much about reality TV.

"After all, it creates more drama if everyone is confined to a small space for an extended period of time," Riley continued.

Her eyes lit. "Yes! You're exactly right. Alastair is all about drama. But Vivian said she needed to talk to me without any cameras. I thought she might have something important to tell me."

"Did she have anything to tell you?" I asked.

"She looked worried—beyond the normal does-Ricky-like-me-the-most-or-not worried. But we didn't even have time to start talking, really, before things went south."

"Do you have any ideas about why she wanted to

talk?" Riley asked.

"No, not really. Maybe to apologize?"

"For what?" I questioned.

"She'd been hurling insults at me and trying to turn the other girls against me. Then she told Ricky how horrible she thought I was. She had the nerve to call me two-faced and said the person Ricky saw wasn't the same one the girls in the house lived with." Joey's frown deepened.

"That had to hurt," I said. Catty women weren't my favorite people to be around. I'd never survive on a show like that.

She nodded. "Vivian was really the one who was two-faced. She acted all high-and-mighty in the house, like she was better than us. But with Ricky she tried to seem like she was a sweetheart without any enemies in the world. I wanted so desperately to tell Ricky that she still talked about her ex-boyfriend back at home."

These women were seriously messed up. But I didn't have the mental energy to go there right now. I had to stay focused.

"Weren't you two worried about getting in trouble?" Riley asked. "Sneaking out could get you kicked off the show."

She shrugged. "I don't know. We're only a week into the show, and at times I want to leave the show and get away from all the drama. I don't really think that's a possibility. I signed a contract . . . and then there's Ricky. I think he likes me."

"And you like him?" I asked, trying to grasp what she was saying.

"Of course. But all of this was too much for me. I don't like sharing my men. It feels unnatural. And, after a while, it seems like it becomes more about winning than it does actually finding love. I mean, when Ricky kissed me for the first time, I thought I was falling in love. But it turns out he's kissed six of us. It makes me feel . . . cheap."

I could only imagine. *Harem* echoed in my head again. That was *not* the way dating should play out.

The old Waylon Jennings' song that served as the show's namesake played like a mental soundtrack in my mind. Which was strange since the tune talked about looking for love in the wrong places and people. Maybe the contestants should take heed of the lyrics and get the hint.

"What happened next on your walk with Vivian?" I asked.

"We were walking down the beach, talking about this stupid competition where we had to eat bugs in order to win a date with Ricky. Mary Ellen won. She's a farm girl from Alabama and not Ricky's type at all, but she was able to stomach those little creepy crawlies." Joey shivered. "Anyway, I saw a boat pull up on the shore as we were talking about the competition, but I didn't really think anything about it. I figured they were probably just night fishing or something."

"What happened next?" I asked.

"The next thing I knew, these men in black had

surrounded us. I guess they came from the boat. It was so dark out there, and I hadn't really thought anything about it. They grabbed Vivian. She was screaming and kicking, but she couldn't get away."

"How many of them were there?" I asked.

"I think four."

"They left you alone during this?" Riley narrowed his eyes in thought.

Joey's chin trembled. "One man tried to grab me, but I ran as fast as I could. After a few minutes, they seemed to forget about me, and they carried Vivian into the water. To their boat, I assume. I couldn't look back. I feel so bad. I left her. How could I have done that? She was kicking and screaming and scared. She was a nasty woman, but I would have never wanted this."

"There was probably nothing you could do to help," I told her.

"They had guns. They seemed militant, you know? I can't put my finger on why exactly. I just felt like these guys were professionals or something."

Interesting observation.

"Was there anything they said to give any indication of who they were or why they took Vivian?" I asked, pondering everything she'd told me. "Accents, tattoos, strange scents even?"

She shook her head. "No, they were quiet. They pretty much just did their job and then left. That was it."

Did their job. That was an odd way to phrase it.

Just then, someone knocked at the door. I looked

out the window and saw the flashing police lights. It was time to hand this over to the professionals.

That's exactly what I planned on doing.

No involvement-o from Gabby-o. That-o was my motto.

***

An hour later, Joey was in the capable hands of the Crystal Key Police Department. Three police officers had shown up. An older man, probably in his early sixties, with a slight build and wrinkle-lined eyes, had talked to us while the rest of his crew went to the beach to look for evidence. Apparently, the chief was out of town and due to arrive back early the next morning.

That meant Riley and I were free to go on with our day.

It was six-thirty now, and Riley and I were wide-awake. And we were on a beautiful island in Florida with nothing to do but relax. That was exactly what I planned on doing.

It always seemed strange to me to continue on with life as if nothing had happened while other people faced tragedies. That was partly why I never did just that. I could help people find answers, heal, and get closure. Why wouldn't I want to do that?

"I don't know about you, but I'm starving. How about we go and grab some breakfast?" Riley pulled me close as we stood in the living room, both still a little shocked from the surprising turn of events.

"Sure thing. But where?"

"There are a few restaurants and shops located within walking distance. I'm sure one of them serves breakfast. I'd offer to cook, but we have no food here yet. We never did make that grocery store run after we got here yesterday."

I nodded, figuring anything I did with Riley would make me happy, especially solving a mystery—I meant, having breakfast together. "Let's go explore."

I donned some white linen pants and a blue T-shirt, along with my favorite flip-flops. I'd bought a new pair just for this trip, so it was a good thing we'd gone somewhere warm where I could wear them. Although, if we'd gone to Alaska, I would have probably worn them anyway. I had this thing for flip-flops. I loved them.

We stepped out into the warm, early morning sunshine. It was already humid outside, and, I couldn't be positive, but I thought I spotted a mosquito swarming around me. In October?

Toto, I've a feeling we're not in Virginia anymore.

Riley's fingers interlaced with mine as we headed toward the sandy, sidewalk-lined street. Palm trees bordered it, as well as other tropical-looking plants that I didn't often see in Virginia. We weren't in the Caribbean, but part of me felt like we were.

And I had to admit that I liked it.

"What a start to our stay, huh?" Riley said.

"I'd say."

I threw one glance over my shoulder at the massive beach house in the distance. Police cars remained there, and a flurry of activity surrounded the place. Officers came and went. Women huddled together. Cameramen filmed it all.

I cleared my throat and ignored my surge of curiosity. "So, who owns this house where we're staying?"

"One of the law partners in the DC office. Mel Murphy."

"That's nice of him to let us use it."

Riley shrugged. "He said there's no reason for it to sit empty. He plans to retire down here."

As soon as we reached the end of the residential street, a row of shops appeared. Most of them were located along the water, and a quaint little boardwalk/pier lined the businesses. Boats were docked along the edges, and waves gently lapped the bulkhead.

The familiar scent of salt water air, mixed with fish and seaweed, carried toward us with the breeze. Early risers walked or jogged on the neat waterfront boardwalk, and several people were already out in boats, kayaks, and paddleboats, enjoying the cooler early morning hours. A few men fished from a pier.

We walked past a bait and tackle shop, a gift store, and a general market. Next we came to Erma's, and, based on the scent of bacon that floated from its open windows, this place served breakfast.

"How's this look?" Riley asked.

"Perfect."

We stepped into the restaurant. Most of the seven other patrons already seated inside had white hair. Fishnets and stuffed marlins and miniature boat replicas lined the walls. It seemed like the kind of place where everyone knew each other. One man even had his bulldog lying on the floor beside him.

"Just two of you?" A woman appeared out of nowhere, menus already in hand. She wore a pink dress with a white apron, and her white hair was coiffed into a beehive. She was adorable. The name "Erma" was embroidered on her lapel.

"Just two," Riley said.

"Right this way." She led us to a table by the window. As I suspected, it was open, allowing the sea breeze to float inside.

As I'd said earlier—this place was perfect.

"Apparently this area is the retirement mecca of the Gulf Coast," Riley whispered after the waitress left us to look over the menu.

Based on the number of senior citizens I'd already seen in our short stay, I'd agree.

We glanced at the menu and, a moment later, Riley ordered an omelet and I ordered eggs, bacon, and fruit. The waitress brought us coffee and water, asked us where we were from, and then moved on to talk to another table.

Riley leaned back, looking more relaxed than I'd seen him in a long time. "So, there are any number of things we can do while we're in the area. There are airboat rides and kayaking. There's swimming in natural springs. Picking oranges. We could even wrestle an alligator." He wiggled his eyebrows.

I smiled. "Or we could just hang out on the beach. I did notice there was a hot tub on one of the decks."

His smile mirrored mine. "Or we could do that."

But I will not—absolutely will not—look into the disappearance of Vivian the Reality Show Star.

I stared out at the water and let my thoughts drift along with the tide.

How had someone known the girls were going to be out on the beach last night? If this was a planned abduction, someone would have had to have known about their impromptu walk. But that was the problem, wasn't it? No one could have known about it if it was spontaneous.

According to Joey, the whole walk and conversation had been Vivian's idea. Did she have something to do with her own abduction?

Joey had said she looked terrified, though. Was the woman a great actress? Or had something gone terribly wrong?

"You're fascinated with what happened last night, aren't you?"

I snapped back to the present and stared at my handsome husband as he sat across the table from me. He'd caught me. I'd promised to stay out of things, and I needed to honor that.

"You're the only thing that fascinates me," I

murmured.

He flashed a smile, but I could tell he wasn't totally convinced of my words as he raised his eyebrows. "That was sweet, but I know you better than that."

I lifted my hands in mock offense. "No, I am perfectly capable of keeping my nose out of other people's business and concentrating solely on my relationships for a week."

"Of course, you are. It's not your fault these situations always pop up wherever you go."

"Exactly! It's not like I seek them out." Finally— Riley understood. A strange burst of contentment filled my chest.

He raised his coffee mug. "It's like God himself puts you in the right place at the right time."

"Yes—exactly!" My thoughts ground to a halt. "Wait—what?"

Riley paused with the cup raised near his chin. "You heard me. Your God-given calling is to be nosy."

I leaned closer and lowered my voice, trying to sound mockingly sultry. "Wow. You've never sounded so attractive."

He let out an all-out laugh and threw his head back. "I don't know what to say to that. You always surprise me."

I reached across the table and grabbed his hand, turning from playful to serious. "I really am thankful for you, Riley. That is sincere."

He squeezed my hand. "I'm thankful for you too.

Life will never be boring with you at my side. I've now got sunshine on a cloudy day." He burst into the song that used those lyrics.

"I'm rubbing off on you! You have no idea how that totally makes me feel like I won a Tony."

"I'm so proud of you that you're not getting involved in this mystery, though. I know that takes a lot of fortitude."

I swallowed back a touch of guilt. If he only knew how much I was struggling inside.

Just then, two older men walked into the restaurant. Both wore Hawaiian shirts and plaid shorts. One was tall and thin, and the other short and rather pudgy. The way they walked and talked together made me think they were old fishing or golfing pals.

"You hear about all the excitement down on the beach last night?" the tall one said to the other as they slid into the booth behind Riley.

I had a bird's-eye view of their conversation, which secretly thrilled me. It all went back to that God-given calling to be nosy.

"An abduction. Sounds like just the perfect storyline for those Hollywood types who are in town," the other said. "I knew there was going to be trouble when I heard they were filming here. Do you remember what I said? I said, 'Mark my words, this will be trouble.' And it is."

"You mark every word you say," his tall companion added, an edge of teasing condescension in his voice.

"Erma, will you get us some coffee and whatever today's special is?" the short one said. "It's on me today because Larry says I never pay. I need to prove him wrong." He paused before adding, "mark my words."

Larry groaned. "You think you're so funny."

"What happened? I heard the police were down there at the Spellman estate." Erma joined their conversation, holding what appeared to be Riley's and my food in her hands. Our eggs were getting colder than a corpse by the second, but I really didn't care.

"It's some kind of dating show," Larry said. "One of the girls was snatched by men in a boat with machine guns."

Machine guns? I'd missed that part of the story when Joey talked to us.

"Apparently, they were wearing gorilla costumes," the man continued.

Everyone in the restaurant seemed to stop eating in order to listen.

"Gorilla costumes—like the ape?" Erma asked, her eyes widening.

"Yep, like the ape," Larry said.

Erma shivered. "Scary for that to be happening right on our normally peaceful shores."

"Apparently, the woman who was snatched was loaded," someone else said from the other side of the restaurant. "That's what the tabloids said, at least. That was before she was snatched, 'course."

"So they abducted her for her money?" Erma

asked, still holding our food hostage.

"That's my best guess. I'll get an update from Old Yeller later when he gets back into town."

I smiled at Riley again. Old Yeller? I imagined an old man with faded blond hair and wrinkled skin.

"We ain't had this much excitement around here since Minnie Pearl lost her false teeth down the toilet and then called it a robbery to try and get the insurance money," Larry said.

"It's 'we haven't,' not 'we ain't,'" someone corrected. "No one says we ain't. No one with any culture, at least."

"Where I'm from, we say whatever we want. We don't care about culture."

A senior citizen brawl? This was going to be the most epic vacation ever.

As long as I minded my own business.

Erma finally set our plates on the table, and I ate my cold eggs. However, the conversation around me had been satisfying enough to make up for my less-than-appetizing food.

CHRISTY BARRITT

CHAPTER 3

As we'd eaten our breakfast, the local conversation had turned from the excitement on the beach last night to politics, to what fish were biting, and a mischief maker who had been taking people's boats on joy rides lately.

It was all fascinating to me. Of course, not as fascinating as Vivian's abduction. I tried to put that out of my mind as we walked back to the house.

"What do you say we spend some time on the beach?" Riley asked as he unlocked the front door.

"That sounds great." Some sun, sand, and time with Riley. It was the perfect mix to get my mind off the fiasco taking place at the house beside ours.

As we stepped into the house, I was struck by how beautiful it was. The inside was exquisitely decorated with exotic, imported-looking furniture. The paint colors—all tropical and bright—as well as the finishing touches made the place look exquisite.

I felt as if I'd invaded someone's dream home—and I was loving every minute of it. It sure did beat the eclectic

35

assortment of furniture in my apartment that I'd collected from yard sales and thrift stores.

I tried to imagine having a second home like this, but it seemed beyond the realm of my reality. I'd grown up poor. Combining my income with Riley's still seemed weird, especially since I'd only had myself to depend on for so long. Maybe money wouldn't feel as tight anymore. That remained to be seen.

In front of me, I spotted Joey's blanket rumpled on the couch. I noted the two coffee mugs we'd used still on the table. In some ways, last night seemed like a bad dream.

But it had really happened.

Riley wrapped his arms around me from behind and gently planted a kiss on my neck. He then rested his chin on my shoulder.

"I'm really happy, Gabby," he murmured.

I leaned back into his embrace, and my insides turned to goo. I kept wanting to pinch myself. "Me too."

I started singing "Lucky I'm in Love" by Jason Mraz and Colbie Caillat. To my surprise, Riley joined me.

"I'm sensing a karaoke duet in our future." I giggled.

"Whatever you want, babe. The good news is that we have a lifetime to look forward to being together and taking trips and discovering more adventures."

"Sounds amazing." By adventures, I assumed he meant being a crime-fighting duo together. Before I could make a *Hart to Hart* reference, I heard a creak above me.

Coming from upstairs.

Riley froze. He'd heard it too.

"Stay here," he told me, his stiff muscles releasing me from our embrace.

"Riley . . ." My muscles tightened with anticipation. I wanted to believe it was just the house settling. My gut told me it wasn't, though.

"Promise me," he said. His gaze left no room for questions.

I finally nodded. "Okay."

I wasn't good at sitting back and doing nothing. I didn't even have my cell phone in case I needed to call the police, nor did I have my gun. Both were upstairs, in the very direction where Riley was headed.

Please, Lord. Protect him. Let it be a bird. A mouse even. I'd take a rat.

But not danger. Not real danger.

I didn't want to begin my life with Riley only to have it end. I'd struggled with the fear since Riley had come back into my life after an encounter with a serial killer had left him on the brink of death.

I stopped and listened. Silence stretched upstairs. I imagined Riley creeping around, looking for the source of the noise. I prayed no one was lying in wait for him.

Visions of what happened on the beach last night filled my mind. Machine guns. Gorilla costumes. An abduction.

What if we'd arrived here just in time for a nightmare to begin in this town?

Just then I heard a loud "Hey!" followed by footsteps pounding above me. My heart leapt into my throat.

Riley . . .

I started to dart toward the sound, but then I remembered my promise to Riley. It seemed like a horrible start to a marriage to break a promise.

But what if he needs me? I should go. Help him. The urgency of the matter trumps my promise . . . right?

My nails dug into the plaster wall behind me as my mental war raged.

More footsteps sounded, along with a shout.

That did it. I was going.

Just as I pushed myself off the wall, Riley thundered down the stairs.

My heart slowed.

He was okay.

I darted to him. "What happened?"

"There was a man upstairs," Riley said. "He jumped from the window and disappeared on the beach. I almost jumped down after him, but I didn't want to break a leg—especially since I wasn't being threatened. Besides, he was too far ahead of me to catch up."

"Why would someone be upstairs?"

He shook his head. "I have no idea. But I don't like this."

My mind raced, immediately wanting answers. That was just the way my mind worked. "Did you get a look at him?"

Riley shook his head. "He was wearing a black mask. It was hard to tell anything about him at all—not his age, his skin color, or even his hair. I'd guess he was about my height, and he was thin."

In other words, we basically knew nothing. Had trouble followed us from Virginia? I doubted it. A whole new trouble was stirring here.

"How in the world did he get inside?" I asked, mentally retracing our steps to determine if we'd locked up behind us. I was nearly certain we had. Riley and I lived in the city. You just didn't leave your doors unlocked there.

"Your guess is as good as mine."

"We should probably call the police," I finally said, trying to do the responsible thing and leave this in law enforcement's capable hands.

"Yeah. I guess we should. We haven't even been here twenty-four hours, and it looks like we're going to become acquainted with them on a first-name basis."

"Sounds about par for the course."

A secret squeal of delight echoed from somewhere inside my mind.

***

Twenty minutes later, Old Yeller showed up, and we explained to the town's police chief what had happened. I only knew who he was because I saw the word "Yeller" on his uniform, but I was desperately curious to know the background on his name.

39

The man looked nothing like I'd envisioned. He was young, with tanned skin and dark hair. His eyes were shifty, making him seem slightly untrustworthy. His tendency to touch his face and hair made him seem nervous.

The three of us stood outside on the deck, where a gentle breeze begged to carry our worries away. If only it were that easy. Another officer looked for clues inside. I resisted the urge to tell him about a great new line of products that could enhance his investigation. I trained people on how to use thus said products for my job with Grayson Tech. But it was better if I kept my mouth shut because that decreased the likelihood of me getting involved in this case.

"So you came back from breakfast and heard a sound upstairs?" Old Yeller repeated, glancing from his notepad to Riley and me and then back down again.

"That's correct." Riley placed his hands on his hips. "The man was upstairs in one of the bedrooms."

"Was anything taken?"

"Not that we can tell," Riley said.

"Maybe you got here early and scared him away," Yeller said.

"No one was supposed to be staying here," I added. "He could have assumed the place was empty . . . except our car was out front. It should have been a dead giveaway."

Had he been watching the house, waiting for us to leave? I shivered at the thought. There were many things I could handle, but being watched creeped me out.

"Maybe we'll find a clue inside that will tell us who this guy is and what he was up to," Yeller said.

Something about the way he said it left me with the impression that he was secretly thinking, *But don't count on it.* He was simply trying to appease us.

I'd glanced upstairs myself before the police arrived and hadn't seen any overwhelming evidence that would point to who did this or what he was up to. Of course, it was hard to tell much because Mr. Murphy had left his own items here. If something had been taken, it would be hard to ascertain what. My guess was that the intruder hadn't been here that long when we'd arrived.

I wasn't ready for this conversation with Chief Yeller to be finished yet. I still had more questions, but I needed to appear unassuming and normal—two words that rarely described me. Standing with my arms crossed and eyes narrowed as if I was about to begin a cross-examination probably wouldn't do me any favors.

I rested one of my hands against a turquoise Adirondack chair beside me. "Chief, is this in any way tied in with what happened on the beach last night? You know . . . the woman who was abducted."

"Why would it be?" Yeller scratched his head, leaving a dark lock out of place.

I took a long sip of water from one of the cups I'd filled for all of us earlier. The day was already heating up— in more ways than one. The action also allowed me to measure my words and actions and to hopefully subdue my impatience.

"Well, how often do crimes occur on the island?" I continued.

He shrugged. "Not often."

"But you've had two crimes in less than twenty-four hours and both have occurred within one hundred feet of this house." Riley narrowed his eyes in thought. "You don't think there's a connection?"

The chief blinked. "Well, now that you put it that way . . ."

I decided to play the victim here and brought my voice—and outrage at his seeming incompetence—down a notch. "What's going on? Should I be frightened? I mean, somehow, this man got into the house, and there are no signs of forced entry. Meanwhile, men with machine guns and gorilla costumes were on the beach."

"Machine guns and gorilla costumes? You must have been listening to the townspeople shooting the breeze. They always like to exaggerate."

"Should I be frightened?" I repeated.

Yeller shifted as if uncomfortable. "We're still trying to figure things out, ma'am. The good news is that the intruder didn't seem to have malicious intent."

I leaned closer and lowered my voice. "Can you tell me this, at least: Are random abductions normal for this area? Do you have any idea what happened to that woman last night? Should I be frightened to be on the beach alone?"

He stared at me stoically, like my questions tested

his patience. "We don't know anything yet. We're still working on it. And this is generally an extremely safe community, so I wouldn't let this interrupt your vacation plans."

Riley pulled me closer. "This is not the way we planned on spending our honeymoon."

Yeller raised his chin. "I understand that, sir. I assure you that we're working hard to find some answers."

"I fear this is all connected with that show being filmed next door." I crossed my arms, fishing for answers. What did Yeller know that I didn't? What I wouldn't do to go over there and question everyone myself . . .

"Again, we're not sure. There's no evidence at this point that these crimes are connected with the show." He rubbed his forehead again. "Now, about this break-in at your place . . ."

CHAPTER 4

No sooner had Old Yeller left than did Wally appear on the sand below. He watched the chief leave, an almost amused look in his eyes.

"You get to talk to the police again?" he said from down below. "Lucky you."

"I suppose," Riley said. "What can we do for you?"

He squinted up at us, still sporting that *Miami Vice* vibe in his sports coat and sunglasses. "Do you mind if I come up for a minute? Or would you both come down?"

"We'll be right there," Riley said, before muttering to me, "What's one more interruption to our trip?"

I could tell he was getting frustrated, and I felt badly about it. He'd worked hard to plan this, and nothing seemed to be working out as he'd envisioned.

We met Wally at the back door.

"Everything okay?" Wally pulled his sunglasses down on his nose as he looked back-and-forth from Riley to me. "I saw the police activity outside."

"Just a little break-in," I said.

His eyebrows shot up. "Break-in? Maybe we should do a better job scouting our locations for *Looking for Love*. I feel like we should be filming *CSI* or one of those other crime dramas. Anyway, I wanted to know if you'd had a chance to look at that contract I left yesterday . . ."

I couldn't hold my tongue. "You're still worried about that? One of your contestants is missing!"

He put on an overly animated expression of sorrow. "Of course, we're concerned about Vivian. Deeply concerned. We're doing everything we can to get her back. But we also have a business here. Time is money when you're working on these shows, and we're already over budget. Ricky's agent knows how to get a good cash advance."

"He has an agent?" I asked. "So he's an actor, not some guy off the street who wants to find his soul mate?"

I really shouldn't have been surprised by that fact. It was just that I'd only recently started to believe in love again, and I hated to see people being fooled by cheap imitations of the real thing.

Wally scoffed. "No, of course not. He's looking for love."

I doubted that. I wondered how many of the women were also actresses. Reality TV wasn't grounded in any reality at all.

"I'm surprised you're still filming," I said, not ready to let this drop.

"We're not. Not right now. We're going dark for at least twenty-four hours to be respectful."

"And after that?"

"After that, we'll have to see. Vivian would want the show to go on."

Uh huh. I was sure she would. I mean, most reasonable people would want others to forget about them and what happened to them after a dramatic abduction in which there was no resolution. I kept my sarcasm at bay.

"How's Joey?" I asked, remembering how upset she'd seemed.

His jaw flexed. "Joey's hanging in. We brought in a masseuse to help the ladies cope."

"A masseuse? What about a counselor?" Riley asked.

"Oh, one of those too. *Of course.* But to these women . . . everything is better with some wine, pampering, and a lot of air time." He let out a clipped laugh before clapping his hands. "So, about those release forms . . ."

I shook my head. Riley and I hadn't even talked about it—we'd all but forgotten about them with the excitement—but the answer was a no brainer, and I felt certain Riley would agree. "We're not signing. I don't want to be connected with this show in any way, shape, or form."

"Are you sure? There could be some compensation involved . . ." His voice lilted upward, as if money might tempt us.

"We're not interested," Riley confirmed.

"Especially not now that a woman is missing."

He stared at us another moment before nodding coldly. "Your loss."

As we watched him walk away, a cold, hard stone seemed to form in my gut.

If that was show business, I wanted no part of it.

***

After Wally left, Riley and I walked down to the general market and bought a few groceries for the week. We came home, ate lunch—sandwiches—and then we headed out to the beach.

The owner had left beachy items—chairs, umbrellas, and inner tubes. We enjoyed the water for a while before drying off in the sun. Riley had brought a Tom Clancy novel to read, and I'd picked up a magazine at the store. It was *Star Touch*, one of those gossipy tabloids. It wasn't usually my first choice in reading, but this issue just happened to be all about *Looking for Love*.

As the sun warmed my skin, I turned over on my blanket and stared at the pictures of the various contestants. My gaze went to Vivian first. She was classically beautiful with an upturned nose, dark hair swept back from her face, and a slender build. The article listed her as a flight attendant who was twenty-four years old and from Southern California.

Beside her was Joey's photo. She was a twenty-five-year-old schoolteacher who enjoyed small town fairs, cow-tipping, and tractor races. She came from a large family and loved dogs.

I scanned the rest of the contestants. As typical for these shows, the producers had cast a tomboy, the life of the party, the sweetheart, and the older woman.

The bulk of the article was about the show's star, Ricky Stamos. Ricky owned a successful bar in Texas. He was thirty-two years old, and he'd never been married. He had a movie-star smile, and, just looking at his pictures, I could tell he had swagger.

"Anything interesting?" Riley asked, putting his book down for a minute.

"Not really. Just trying to relax."

He looked over my shoulder. "By reading about the show being filmed next door?"

I shrugged. "Coincidental."

His "uh huh" clearly stated that he didn't believe me.

"The first episode comes on tonight . . ." I added.

He pulled down his sunglasses. "Please don't tell me you want to watch it."

"You don't?" I batted my lashes innocently.

"It will only build your interest in this case."

I shook my head, trying to convince myself as much as I wanted to convince him. "No interest. You're crazy."

He gave me another skeptical, "Uh huh."

I turned back to the magazine. "Now, if you'll excuse me, I'm going to soak up some sun."

"Do you need more sunscreen?"

"I'm fine."

"You sure?" he asked. "I've heard it's easier to get burned the farther south you go."

I waved him off. "I grew up at the beach. I'm fine."

Just because I had fair skin and red hair and burned easily as a child shouldn't be a matter of concern. I'd slathered sunscreen on when I'd gotten out of the water. Besides, one of the articles in *Star Touch* was about how toxic sunscreen could be. I'd been in the sun all summer, so it wasn't like my skin was still fresh and untouched.

I turned back to the magazine and studied the various contestants.

What kind of self-respecting man or woman would go on a show like this? Were some people actually sincere in their desire to meet the love of their lives? Or was this a matter of desiring fifteen minutes of fame?

Why were women abducted?

Serial killer? I sure hoped not.

Human trafficking? Oh, Lord, please no.

As leverage by someone relying on the goodwill and concern of loved ones? Possibly, but as far as I knew there was no ransom note yet.

Certainly there were other reasons, but what?

It didn't take long for my thoughts to go back to Vivian. What could have happened to her? Had she staged her abduction? Had the show staged it? Was she secretly rich royalty?

The crime seemed so strange. So strange because it appeared there was no way it could have been premeditated. Not when the walk was spontaneous.

Halfway through my ponderings, I felt a shadow block my UV rays.

I looked up and spotted a man dressed in cargo shorts and a casual button-up top standing over me. He wore sunglasses and had spiky blond hair that used more gel than a high school production of *Grease*.

He had to be with the show. He looked like the showbiz type.

"Excuse me," he started. "You two are the ones using this home this week, correct? I was hoping to ask you both a few questions. Sorry to interrupt your fun."

I sat up and exchanged a quick look with Riley.

"Who are you?" Riley put his book down and bristled.

I'd lost count of how many interruptions we'd had so far in our time here. Was this the third? If I included Joey, it would be the fourth . . . maybe. Why couldn't people just leave us alone?

The man flashed a smile, and I was pretty sure his teeth were so white and shiny that only my sunglasses had protected my eyes. "I'm Trevor McManus with Elite Security. My associates and I have been hired to look into the abduction of Vivian Gray."

"Elite Security?" I questioned. The man had my full attention.

"We're a private investigation firm based out of Miami."

"And you came all the way out here in order to

work this case?" I clarified

"The show wanted to hire only the best. That would be Elite. I can humbly say that we're the cream of the crop. Ex cops, military, Special Forces. You name it." He flashed his award-winning smile again.

"What can we do for you?" Riley asked.

"I was hoping to ask you some questions. I understand you talked to Joey last night."

"That's correct," I said. "We were the closest house so she ran over, trying to escape from the men." I eyed him suspiciously. "What's this have to do with anything?"

"Can you recount exactly what she told you?"

I didn't see where it would do any harm, so I launched into what had happened. Leaving this investigation in someone else's capable hands seemed like the perfect way for me to let it go and avoid any more of these interruptions. They could single-handedly save our honeymoon.

The man nodded as I talked, taking some notes on a pad of paper.

"Did either of you see anything? Did you happen to spot the boat on the water?" he asked.

I shook my head. "No, we were sleeping up until the moment Joey pounded on our door."

He tapped his pen against the paper and nodded. "Thank you. You've been very helpful. Here's my card in case you remember anything."

I took it and used it as a placeholder in my magazine.

"Any word on Vivian?" I asked. Maybe I should use the role of innocent, frightened bystander more often. It seemed so much less assuming than pushy investigator. Maybe I'd been approaching getting answers the wrong way all along.

"No, not yet."

"That poor girl's family," I continued. "No ransom demands."

"No, ma'am." His expression showed nothing. Nothing." He shifted. "Well, have a nice day. Oh, and you might want to put on some sunscreen, ma'am. Your back is looking a little burnt."

***

"Your skin is the same color as the siding of the house, Gabby." Riley squinted as if just looking at my back caused him pain.

"You're so romantic," I murmured as I stared with contempt at myself in the bathroom mirror.

Riley stood behind me. We'd just come inside after being at the beach for most of the day. My hair was windblown and crazy. Irritating sand clung to my legs and feet. But those things were nothing compared to my skin. My very, very red skin.

I attempted to move the strap of my bathing suit a couple inches so I could see for myself how bad the damage was, but just touching it caused my skin to revolt in a major *owie* moment. Not only that, but my sunglasses had left white circles around my eyes, and I looked like some kind of oddly colored raccoon.

"How did this happen?" I muttered, staring at the stark white line as it contrasted with the crimson of my skin. I looked like an American flag. I just needed to paint my face blue and add some white stars.

"Lack of sunscreen?"

"I put some on!" Bless his heart for not saying, "I told you so," when he had every right to. He'd asked me if I should reapply it at least three times, but I'd ignored him.

Riley shrugged. "You're not one who usually sits out sunbathing. Maybe you forgot how much sun you could handle."

"I usually don't have time to sit and do nothing." I resisted the urge to touch my skin again and wallow in the pain I'd caused myself. "I haven't spent that much time on the beach since I was a teenager."

He stared at my back and frowned. "I hope it doesn't blister."

Wasn't this just great? A sunburn on my honeymoon. That might put a damper on things.

"Look, how about this?" Riley started to rest his hands on my shoulders but stopped himself. "I'll run to get some aloe and pick up something to eat. We can stay in tonight and watch a movie or something. Maybe by tomorrow your skin will feel better."

I nodded, knowing he was being kindly optimistic. "Sounds good. I'll get cleaned up while you're gone."

After he left, I washed off all the sand. Even the

SWEPT AWAY

cool water hitting my skin made fire shoot through me. Toweling off had been excruciating. Staying naked seemed preferable to getting dressed, but I wasn't the type. What had I been thinking?

I knew exactly what had happened: I'd gotten distracted with thoughts of the mystery playing out around me and had neglected my poor skin and all my sensibilities.

By the time I carefully put on some sweatpants and one of Riley's T-shirts—one of my most unattractive outfits and not what I'd planned on wearing for my honeymoon—Riley was back. He'd brought some soup and salads from a nearby deli.

We sat down in front of the TV to eat, and I hoped this wasn't a glimpse into our future. When we turned it on, *Looking for Love* played out across the screen. I hated to admit it, but my heart raced when I realized what it was.

"I didn't think they aired reality shows until they were finished filming the whole season," I muttered.

"*Looking for Love* is a little different in that everything airs a week after it's filmed. It cuts down on the amount of editing that takes place," Riley said before eating a spoonful of his seafood chowder.

I wasn't sure how he knew that, but maybe it was common knowledge and I was clueless.

"I can't believe they're airing this after everything that's happened . . ." It seemed so insensitive. Despite that, I couldn't take my eyes off the screen.

The opening episode had the cast meeting Ricky for the first time at a fancy mansion in LA. Just as I'd thought, Ricky came across as the guy every woman wanted. He was handsome and charming and said all the right things to make the ladies swoon.

He wasn't the settling down type. That was plain for anyone to see. It didn't matter how many times he said otherwise on the screen. I knew because I'd met his type before. I'd dated his type before, for that matter.

When Vivian came on the screen, my heart jerked into my throat. She was just as beautiful as I'd imagined, with classic good looks. I watched carefully, noting how she was demure and sweet around Ricky. As soon as she was around only the women, however, she became aloof and snotty.

"Maybe Joey was telling the truth," Riley said.

"Or it could all be in the editing." I tried to eat my soup, but I was too hot. I decided to pick at my salad instead.

"True."

The camera panned to Joey, who stood in the background at the meet and greet, giving an ice-cold glare to Vivian. It was more than that, though. Joey seemed nervous. Her gaze skittered around when she was alone. As soon as someone talked to her, she turned into the girl-next-door whom Riley and I had met.

Interesting.

When the show cut from the screen, Wally came on to tell viewers about what happened to Vivian. He urged anyone with any information to call a number on the screen. They were also offering a reward for anyone who knew anything. At least the show had the decency to do that.

"Can you imagine if our dating life had been aired for everyone to see?" Riley asked, putting his empty bowl on the coffee table.

"That would have been horrible. We would have never survived. Love is hard enough without an audience critiquing every word, action, and possible ulterior motive."

"It's true. Some things should just be private. Add to that the way these people are edited—they become more of a character than a person. They fall in love in the most extraordinary of circumstances, a reality that real life can never replicate."

Our dating story hadn't been smooth, and it had been filled with many ups and downs. But the downtimes had taught us the most about each other's characters.

"You have to learn how to love when the going gets tough," I said. "It's easy to love in the good, extravagant times."

"I agree."

I leaned forward and kissed his lips.

He reached to pull me closer, but when his hands hit my back, I nearly jumped off the couch as fire spread across my skin.

"Sorry," I muttered. "But I may have single-handedly ruined our honeymoon."

Or my preoccupation with the case had, at least. Which still meant that I'd ruined it.

When would I ever learn?

***

The next morning, the doorbell awoke us.

I buried my head under the pillow and immediately gasped as it hit my shoulders. Sunburns stunk. Sunburns on honeymoons stunk. People showing up at the house whenever they wanted stunk.

Riley groaned beside me. "This place is Grand Central Station. Why can't people leave us alone?"

"Tell me about it."

A few minutes later, we scurried downstairs and pulled the front door open. Old Yeller stood there.

"Can we help you?" Riley said.

Chief Yeller looked serious—there were no smiles or friendly greetings to be seen, nor was he touching his hair and face nervously. He did blanch when he saw me, however. Must have been my raccoon eyes.

"Mr. and Mrs. Thomas, can I come inside a moment?" he started.

Riley glanced at me before pulling the door all the way open and stepping back. The lines on his face looked tight and drawn, like he was anticipating the worst. "Sure."

Old Yeller stepped inside and held up a paper. "I have a warrant to search the premises."

"On what grounds?" Riley asked, snatching the

paper from his hands.

"We have evidence connecting this property with the missing woman."

"What . . . ?" I gasped. I hadn't seen that one coming.

"Do you mind?" Yeller nodded behind us.

"Be our guest," Riley swept a hand to the side as an invitation to the police officers who approached.

We moved aside as three other cops also came inside.

"What do you think is going on?" I whispered as the men began opening doors and drawers and looking behind everything possible.

"I have no idea." Riley's gaze remained on the officers.

He looked worried, I realized. There must be some pretty strong evidence for the police to get a warrant to search the property. I couldn't imagine what that might be.

A few minutes later, Yeller came back downstairs, holding an evidence bag with something inside. "You ever seen this before?"

I looked more closely. It was a black sandal.

"I've never seen it," Riley said, before turning toward me. "Is it yours?"

I shook my head. "No, it's not."

Yeller studied us both with a dogged gaze. "Well, it was in the guest bedroom upstairs."

I still didn't see what the big deal was. "Maybe it

belongs to the house's owner, Mr. Murphy. He and his wife kept some of their personal belongings here at the house."

Yeller narrowed his gaze. "This belongs to Vivian."

My eyes widened. Yet another one I hadn't seen coming. "Vivian hasn't been here. Not that I know of, at least. I don't see how that would even be possible. Riley and I have been here almost the whole time."

He lowered his head, almost like he was trying too hard to look tough. "Are you sure about that?"

I nodded, not liking where all of this was going. "Positive."

"I also noticed you have a gun," Yeller continued. "It was in the nightstand in the master bedroom."

"I have a concealed carry permit from Virginia," I told him. "Florida is a reciprocal state—I checked before I left. The permit is in my purse, and I can get it for you if you'd like."

"I would like that."

"Can you tell us what's going on?" Riley asked.

His eyes glimmered as he observed us in a moment of contemplation. "We found the boat used in Vivian McDonald's abduction. It was abandoned up near Caladesi Island."

My heart quickened. "Where's that?"

"Not far from Clearwater and Honeymoon Island State Park."

I wasn't exactly certain where those places were from here, but I assumed they were fairly close. "That's good news, right?"

"She wasn't on board. One of her shoes was." He held up the black sandal he'd found upstairs. "It matches this one."

My quickening heartbeat traveled all the way up to my ears, thumping with a deafening beat.

"You're saying that one of Vivian's shoes was found on the boat and the other in the house? In *this* house?" Riley asked. He sounded as confused as I felt.

"That's exactly what I'm saying," Yeller said. "I'm also saying that the owner of the boat where the shoe was found is also the owner of this house. Would you know anything about that?" He stared at both of us, watching our reactions.

"Absolutely not." Riley's voice took on a lawyerish tone. "We weren't aware Mr. Murphy had a boat, and, even if he did, we weren't entitled to use it."

"I'm going to need to give the house's owner a call to verify that," Yeller said.

"Of course. Go right ahead." Riley spouted off his number.

Yeller dialed his number and, a few seconds later, began muttering in the phone. The conversation was indiscernible from our end, however, filled with lots of grunts and is-that-rights. Anticipation mounted across my back every time Yeller glanced back at us.

When Yeller hung up, he turned toward us. "Mr. Murphy doesn't know anything about anyone staying here. Now, would you care to explain yourself? Or I'd be happy to take you down to the station."

CHAPTER 5

"This is a misunderstanding," Riley said. "Let me talk to him."

"I repeat: he knew nothing about you staying here." Yeller leveled his gaze with us, probably trying to look scary.

"That's ridiculous." Riley's hands flew in the air in an unusual display of frustration. "He gave me the key himself."

"That's not what he said," Yeller countered.

"Seriously, please let me call him," Riley said. "I'm not sure what just happened, but something is wrong. We have permission to stay here."

"We wouldn't be here otherwise," I quipped, feeling like I needed to say something. No way were we taking the fall for this fiasco.

Riley pulled out his phone and quickly dialed. An echo of the earlier conversation happened again: lots of grunts and indiscernible talking. Finally, he hung up and turned to us.

"You didn't talk to Mr. Murphy. You talked to his assistant Mr. *Mercy*."

Yeller didn't say anything for a moment. "I dialed the number you gave me."

"Did you even ask who you were speaking with? Mr. Murphy has a paralegal who is taking all of his calls while Mr. Murphy is at a wedding in India."

Yeller blinked. "I'll need to verify that."

"Please do."

Yeller dialed the number on his phone, and a moment later he confirmed what Riley had said. He hung his hands on his belt and frowned. "Sorry for the misunderstanding."

"Now, do you believe us when we say we have no idea what happened to the boat?" Riley said. "I don't even know where it was docked."

"Down at the local marina," Yeller said.

"I don't have the key to operate the boat." Riley crossed his arms, definitely annoyed.

"We found one on the dresser upstairs. In the bedroom where the shoe was found."

I shook my head as I thought it all through. "Joey ran to our house right after Vivian was abducted. We couldn't have been in the boat and made it back here to meet Joey, if we were the ones in the boat."

"Now that I might believe. But that still doesn't explain how the shoe ended up here."

"Did you forget that someone broke into our house yesterday?" Riley reminded him.

Yeller scratched his eyebrow. "That's true."

"Whoever broke in must have planted that shoe, hoping we'd look guilty," I muttered, not liking the conclusions I drew.

"Why would someone do that?" Yeller asked, doing the head-scratching thing again.

"To take suspicion off themselves, of course!" I nearly threw my hands in the air. I wasn't one who thought small town cops couldn't cut it. Not at all. But this guy needed some help.

"Interesting theory."

I fought a sigh. "Is there any sign of Vivian? That's the important thing."

His shoulders drooped. He knew he was in over his head, didn't he? "No, not yet."

"I left a voicemail for Mr. Murphy," Riley said. "He's supposed to call me back when he gets the message, but, like I said, he's in India. I want to ask him who else had access to his boat."

"Smart idea," Yeller said. "Because I'm not leaving here until I know something."

***

Mr. Murphy called back an hour later and confirmed we were allowed to stay here. He also said that he'd let several people use the house over the years, but no one else should have a key or permission to use his boat. He did mention that he had a son with drug problems, who occasionally turned up here.

He'd apologized profusely for the trouble.

But that still didn't explain why someone had left the shoe here. I mean, obviously they wanted to make us look guilty. But why target Riley and me? Why leave one shoe?

Unless they had to leave the other shoe on the boat so the chief would connect the dots.

That would be pretty calculated, which these guys very well could be. After all, they had somehow managed to snag a woman off the beach when she wasn't supposed to be there.

And then there were the bigger questions like: Where was Vivian? Why had she been taken? And who was behind it?

After everything that happened this morning, Riley and I decided to go into town for lunch at Erma's. When we got there, all the locals were talking about the boat. Apparently, they'd heard about what happened with Mr. Murphy's watercraft before the police even finished questioning us at the house.

Small town dynamics were something I wasn't used to.

A few of the restaurant's regulars sent guilty looks back at Riley and me, like they knew who we were but didn't really care that they were talking about us. That was just as well.

"Do you think someone is trying to set us up?" Riley whispered.

"That's what it looks like. Why else would he have left that shoe?" I'd been thinking about it since it happened.

"I just don't understand why. Why target us?"

I shook my head. "At this point, I have no idea."

Riley stared out the window. The boardwalk out front was considerably busier today than it was yesterday morning. Numerous people walked about, shooting the breeze or eating ice cream or carrying fishing poles.

This really was such a lovely place. It was too bad our stay here had been marred by Vivian's abduction, *Looking for Love*, and Yeller's accusations. The locale had so much potential for relaxation.

Suddenly, Riley sat straight up, his gaze fixated outside. "Gabby, do you see that?"

I straightened also, anticipation buzzing through me. "See what?"

"Him." He nodded to someone in the distance.

I tried unsuccessfully to follow his gaze. I saw a lot of people, but no one who stood out as someone to watch. "Who?"

Riley's gaze was latched out the window still, and his body language screamed, "alert." "Vince Daley."

I still wasn't following this, which annoyed me because I hated feeling confused. "Who is Vince Daley?"

I figured the guy he was talking about had to be the younger-looking man with light-brown hair who was headed toward the marina. He was the only person who stood out among the crowd. Something about the way he moved made him look shady, like he was up to something.

"Vince Daley was on *Looking for Love* last season."

Now Riley had my full attention. I mean, he'd had it before. But now he *really* had it.

"That guy out there was on last season?" I echoed, making sure I understood this correctly.

"He was the runner-up, but he wasn't chosen by Katrina at the end." Riley cleared his throat, and his cheeks reddened slightly. "That's what I've heard, at least."

My curiosity was fully aroused now. "What else did you hear?"

Riley continued staring outside, his every muscle looking like he was prepared to jump into action. "Everyone expected him to be the next Mr. Eligible, but Ricky was chosen instead. Rumor has it that Vince was really angry about it."

How did Riley know these details? This had to go beyond the normal scuttlebutt that people heard on the tube about various TV shows.

There was something my husband wasn't telling me. Was he secretly a fan of *Looking for Love*?

I stared at him until he cringed.

"What?" Riley shrugged, looking a little too innocent.

"How do you know all of that?" I tilted my head as I began my mini cross-examination.

He cringed again and raised his shoulders in a half-shrug. "I just . . . heard about it when I left the TV on once."

I nodded slowly, unconvinced. "Is that right?"

"Of course. You don't think I watch *Looking for Love*, do you?" He laughed a little too loudly.

I knew him well enough to know there was something he wasn't telling me. "You seem to know an awful lot about the show."

He looked out the window again. "That's not important right now. What's important is the fact that Vince is in town. Why would he be here?"

I cast aside my interrogation, knowing I'd pick it up again later. Riley was right—we had other more important matters to focus on. "Maybe the show invited him out for one of those ambush episodes. I've heard they like the shock factor. And, in full disclosure, I have watched two whole episodes before."

He ignored my comment. "You're right—his presence here could be a stunt of some sort. But he's heading toward the marina, and I don't see any camera crews following him. In fact, he's kind of looking around, like he doesn't want to be spotted."

Our gazes connected.

"Should we follow him?" I asked.

"I think that's a good idea. Especially since someone is trying to make us look guilty. It couldn't hurt to clear our names before this really does become a nightmare honeymoon."

"Let's go."

We both stood, and, as I passed the waitress, I told her we'd be right back for our food, which we'd take to go.

We stepped outside into the humid air and took off toward the marina. As soon as our feet hit the wooden planks there, Vince hopped into a boat and the driver took off.

"He's going to get away," Riley muttered.

We picked up our pace, trying to reach him in time, but it was too late. They pulled out into the water, waves flying behind them.

Vince looked over his shoulder at us as he cruised farther from the shore.

I couldn't see him well enough to know if he was smirking. But my suspicions were that that was exactly what he was doing.

CHAPTER 6

Riley and I decided to take our food back to the house to eat. It was all packaged up in a neat paper bag and tucked under Riley's arm as we started down the sidewalk. The scent of bacon from my club sandwich and warm french fries drifted through the bag and tantalized my senses, making my stomach growl.

We'd only taken five steps in our quest to head home when a limo pulled up to the curb beside us and women began bouncing out.

The first person I spotted was Joey. And the first person Joey spotted was Riley.

She went right to him. Her eyes immediately became tear-rimmed and drama-filled.

"I was hoping I might see you again," she started.

My back muscles tightened. Was she hitting on him while I was on my honeymoon and while she was on a dating show? That would take some nerve.

A knot formed between Riley's eyebrows as he held her at arm's length. "What's going on?"

"You said you're an attorney, right?" Joey batted her eyelashes.

"That's correct."

"I need to hire you."

Riley shook his head slightly, as if her question threw him. "For what?"

"I'm afraid I'm a suspect in Vivian's disappearance. I expect that the police will bring me in for questioning any time now. I'm not stupid. I know I need representation if that happens, and I don't know any lawyers down here. Except you."

"Why would they bring you in?" I asked.

Joey looked at me for the first time, and her eyes widened with horror. *Raccoon face strikes again.* She quickly recovered and continued on with her dilemma. "I was the last one to be seen with her. I know how all this works. I've watched *Law and Order.*"

"Have the police given you any indication that you're a suspect?" I continued.

"No. Not yet. But give them time."

"I'm only qualified to practice law in Virginia, Joey," Riley told her.

Her lips stuck out in a girly pout. "I didn't think of that. What am I going to do, Riley? I'm not like some of these women who come from gobs of money. My dad's a farmer. I quit my job to come on this show." She shook her head. "I feel so helpless."

Riley was silent a moment until he finally said, "There is someone I went to law school with who lives in this area now."

Her eyes widened. "There is?"

"His name is Devin Matthews. I could call him for you, if you'd like."

"Oh, would you?"

My gaze traveled beyond Joey for a moment. All the bikini-clad women headed toward the marina, acting as if nothing had happened—or that nothing would stand in the way of their fifteen minutes of fame. Maybe I was being too harsh. But how could they continue on after one of their own was abducted? Were they all as happy and carefree as they appeared?

Wally followed behind them, talking with another man—possibly another producer, if I had to guess. Ricky led the pack, and the girls clamored to be beside him. He obviously loved it, based on the grin across his face.

There was also another man. Alastair, I realized. I'd seen his picture in the article in *Star Touch*. He was the one who'd started this franchise. It had really launched his career, which now included several reality shows. Apparently, he was a hands-on kind of guy who liked to be on the set as much as possible.

I came back to the conversation in time to see Joey clasp her hands together in front of her and tilt her head at Riley. "I'm so lucky I met you," she muttered.

Seriously, this woman could win an award for her over-acting.

When she threw her arms around him, I bristled.

Hands off, lady.

"Joey, over here!" one of the other women called.

"We're going parasailing," Joey said. "I've got to run. But I'll be in touch."

I stared at Riley when she left, waiting for his commentary on the conversation that had just played out. He shrugged innocently.

"What?" he finally said.

I decided not to comment on Joey's obvious flirtation with him. After all, I trusted Riley that the feelings weren't reciprocal, even if his wife did look like a raccoon.

Besides, I had another more pressing thought. "Vince just took a boat out. Now the girls are going. Coincidence?"

Riley shook his head. "Probably not. What do you say we charter a boat and keep an eye on things?"

My heart rate quickened. "Really?"

He shrugged. "Let's face it: neither of us is good at doing nothing. Besides, these girls could be in danger, and someone's trying to frame us for it."

A huge grin stretched across my face. "Let's do it."

***

To our surprise, we were able to charter a little boat to take us into the Gulf. Unfortunately, it was a fishing boat, and I had no desire to fish. But it was worth it if it meant keeping an eye on what was going on. Wally and Alastair certainly didn't seem to care, and Chief Yeller seemed unable to comprehend the scope of this investigation.

Our "captains" were none other than Larry and Leonard, the two men we'd heard talking at Erma's the first morning. I thought it was a nice twist of fate—or should I say "faith"?—that these two talkers would be our guides.

As we set off into the Gulf, my oversized white-linen shirt billowed in the breeze. Riley wrapped his arm around the back of the bench seat where we sat at the rear of the boat. I wanted to lean into him, but I didn't dare.

And I knew what was coming next: peeling. I was going to look *so* attractive when that started. I'd move from looking like a tomato to looking like an orange without the rind. Oh joy.

"So, let's get back to that earlier *Looking for Love* discussion," I started, talking over the roar of the motor as we cruised across the water. "You watch the show, don't you? You more than watch it. You *like* it."

He didn't say anything for a moment, but a slight smile played on his lips. Until finally he nodded and raised a hand in surrender. "You caught me. I started watching it when I moved back home to my parents while I was recovering. I became addicted."

"I knew it!"

"It's a guilty pleasure," he continued. "One I'm not very proud of."

"It just goes to prove that even Riley Thomas isn't perfect."

"I thought we'd drawn that conclusion a long time ago."

I reached up and pecked his lips in a kiss. "Believe it or not, I love that you're not perfect. If you were, I'd feel unworthy to be married to you."

"I guess we're a pair then."

"You two on your honeymoon?" Leonard asked.

I nodded. "Yes, we are."

"I figured as much. You two have that look about you. My Elsa and I had that look at one time. She passed away eight years ago. Heart disease."

"I'm sorry to hear that," I said.

"Marriage was the best thing to ever happen to me," he continued. "Treasure each other. Even when the going gets tough. There will come a time when you're tempted to give up. Don't do it. Anything worth having is worth working for. Mark my words."

I smiled and tucked away his wisdom. "I think you're right. Thanks for the advice."

"It's free. One of the few things in life that are." He chuckled.

I shifted. "Leonard, can you tell us about Old Yeller?" I was still dwelling on how competent—or not— the police chief was.

Leonard shrugged. "Nice enough guy. One of the few true locals around here. Most of us are retired, in case you didn't know. But his family grew up on the north end. His mom ran the local market, and his father worked for the state, commuting to and from work."

"How'd he get the nickname?" I asked.

"I guess he was always an old soul—maybe it had to do with hanging around all of us. He liked to play checkers and do crossword puzzles. The nickname started down at his mom's market, and it stuck."

"Does he do a good job as police chief?" I asked.

"For the crimes we have around here, sure. It's not much, though. He checks boating permits, handles out-of-control parties sometimes, gives speeding tickets. Nothing exciting like that abduction the other night."

As the conversation tapered, my gaze was pulled to another boat in the distance. "Riley, check that out."

He followed my gaze. A little boat, like the one Vince had jumped on, bobbed in the distance. Was it Vince? And, if so, what was he planning?

"Stop here!" Riley yelled.

Larry slowed before stopping. "You want to anchor here and see if anything is biting?"

"Uh . . . sure," Riley said. "It looks like as good an area as any."

The girls parasailed in the distance, but I thought we were far enough away that we wouldn't draw any attention.

"You two aren't moving very quickly," Leonard said, staring at us. "Don't you want to catch your own fish, scale it yourself, and eat it tonight for dinner? Nothing more satisfying."

Um . . .no, not really.

"Maybe we'll just sit here and enjoy the moment,"

Riley said.

"Hmm," Larry said. "Whatever you want. But I did hear that grouper are biting." Larry paused. "Heard about Murphy's boat."

I let Riley take lead on this one. "Someone took it for a joy ride."

"Police came out and searched the place, huh?" Leonard added.

"It's true," Riley said. "But we didn't have anything to do with that abduction. We're not sure what's going on or how anyone got that boat."

"Hope everything works out," Larry said.

"So do we." Riley still stared across the water. "You take many people out fishing like this?"

"My fair share. Had lots of visitors in town lately. An unusual number."

My curiosity spiked. "Any idea why?"

"Not really. Suppose it could be because of this show. Some people like to come out and gawk. But I've had several inquires this week."

"Did you get any from a group of men, by chance? Younger, kind of slick acting," I said.

"Nope."

My hopes fell.

"But my friend Cecil did," Larry continued, staring across the expanse of water.

I glanced at Riley before saying, "Is that right?"

Larry nodded. "Yep. It sure is. Apparently, they wanted to rent the whole boat, though, instead of letting

Cecil charter it. Cecil didn't want anything to do with that. That boat is his baby."

"I can't blame him," I said. "Did these guys say where they were from?"

"Not sure. You'd have to ask Cecil that."

"When exactly did these guys roll into town?" Riley asked.

"Hmm . . . Probably three days ago."

Riley nudged me and pointed to another boat in the distance. Four men were onboard. Young men. They weren't tubing or doing any other water sports. It was almost like they were scouting out the area. Or trying to keep an eye on the cast of the show.

Joey had said four men had abducted Vivian.

"Larry, would you mind following that boat?" I asked.

"What about fishing?"

"That can wait," I said. "We really want to see the area."

"It's your time. I'll do whatever you want—so long as it's not illegal."

I glanced back one more time at the boat I thought Vince was in. It had disappeared. For the moment, I felt like the girls were safe. I hoped I was right.

I had no idea what Vince was doing, but right now I wanted to check these other guys out.

***

We rounded a small jetty of land and headed around to the north side of the island—away from our house. The men didn't seem to notice us—we were a considerable distance behind them. So far behind that it was hard to tell much about them.

"Can you slow down some?" I asked Larry.

"I understand," he yelled over the motor. "You don't want to be obvious that you're following those guys. That's what you're doing, aren't ya?"

"Between you and me—yes," I said.

We puttered behind them as they went under the causeway bridge, which connected Crystal Key with the mainland, and kept circling the island.

Interesting.

They sped up after rounding the north side of the island. I held my breath, waiting to see where they could go.

As we cleared the curve, an empty waterway stretched before us.

What? Where had they gone?

I stared at a long row of piers and boathouses that stretched along the bay side of the island.

There was no sign of the boat.

"Do you know anything about these houses?" I asked Larry and Leonard.

"Not really. Those are some rentals. I think some doctor owns that one, but he only comes down twice a year. A lawyer owns that one over there. I heard J Lo is buying that one on the end."

I burned as much as I could into my memory. But there were no clues as to where those guys had gone. Maybe into a boathouse. Maybe they'd rounded the island again in an effort to lose us.

There was no way to know for sure, and I didn't even know what else to look for.

Larry glanced at his watch. "Anything else you need? Bingo starts in an hour, and I really don't want to miss it."

***

That night, I lay in bed, wishing I could enjoy Riley's arms around me. But every time the sheets hit my skin, pain burst through me. Since I couldn't sleep, I replayed the events from the day and tried in vain to figure this mystery out.

And it was while my thoughts were racing that I heard a creak downstairs.

Not a the-house-is-settling type of creak.

It sounded like someone was inside.

Was it the same person who'd sneaked in two days ago? Had he come back to finish what he'd started when he left that sandal?

I grabbed my gun from the nightstand. If I woke Riley, he would insist on handling this himself. It might sound crazy, but I wanted to do this on my own. I didn't want to send him downstairs to face someone who could potentially harm him. I'd almost lost him once already.

I tiptoed toward the door and gently nudged it open. Darkness waited for me on the other side.

I paused, listened.

Another creak sounded from downstairs.

After a moment of hesitation, I stepped out. I stayed close to the wall as I crept toward the stairs. My gun remained raised in front of me so I would be ready to act, if needed.

I'd been at the mercy of a killer before, and I'd vowed to never be in that position again. Victim no more.

When I finally reached the first floor, it hit me: Riley was going to kill me.

Guilt washed through me. *What had I been thinking, coming down here alone and not calling the police first? I'm a smart girl. I should know better.*

I'd had some kind of independent impulse, and I'd acted without thinking.

I looked back at the stairs, ready to go back up and call the police like a good girl. With any luck, Riley would never know I'd left.

Before I could move, a shadow stepped from around the corner.

CHAPTER 7

"Whoa! Who're you?" the man in front of me slurred.

I pointed my gun and tried to steady my trembling hands. "Who are you?"

"I . . . live . . . here." The man crossed his arms, as if daring me to defy him.

"You are not Mr. Murphy," I muttered.

I didn't know Mr. Murphy, but this man didn't strike me as an attorney on the verge of retirement. This man was probably twenty-something, and the distinct scent of alcohol saturated every inch of him. He had longish, sun-bleached hair with nasty dreads. His body looked bony, and his skin had scattered sores.

Meth addict? It was a good possibility.

"I most certainly am. I am Mr. Murphy!" The man raised a finger in the air with an inebriated flamboyance. "And you are trespassing on my property."

Just then someone thundered down the stairs, stopping halfway. Probably when he'd seen both the stranger and my gun.

"Gabby?"

Riley.

My heart sank.

"I've got this," I muttered, still holding my gun and trying to look tougher than I felt.

"What's going on?" He slowly and cautiously continued to the bottom. His gaze wavered from me to the man on the other end of my gun. "Who are you?"

"This man broke into the house," I announced, my gun still pointed at the supposed Mr. Murphy. Honestly, I figured he was harmless, but I wasn't taking any chances.

I could feel Riley's gaze boring into me. "And you came down to confront him and left me sleeping?"

"Not my smartest move. Sorry." My words were sincere, but I didn't have time to grovel right now or explain that this self-sufficient girl might have some trouble operating as a team.

Riley's gaze continued to sear into me—a mix of righteous anger and hurt—until he finally turned toward the man in front of me. I knew we'd have an uncomfortable conversation later. I wasn't looking forward to it.

"You are not Mr. Mel Murphy," Riley said.

"I beg to differ. I am Mr. Homer Murphy." He let out a slight bow, as if he were royalty. As he did so, he accidentally hit a vase on the table beside him and sent it shattering on the floor.

"You're his son," I muttered, putting things together.

The one who's a drug addict.

He pointed at me and pursed his lips. "You're on the nose." He tried to touch his nose, but poked his eye instead. "And you are . . . ?"

Riley stepped forward, gently edging me behind him while still keeping the gun pointed at Homer. "I work with your father. He said we could use this place for our honeymoon."

"Aw . . . wasn't that nice of him?" His sickly sweet smile disappeared. He tried to lean on the high table beside him, only to knock it down also. He straightened. "The only problem is that I need to use it."

"Were you the one who was in here two days ago?" Riley narrowed his eyes as he stared at the man.

"That was you?" Homer twisted his lips in confusion.

"That was us," Riley said. "I saw you. You were wearing a mask. And you ran. Those aren't the actions of someone who's innocent or of someone who's supposed to be staying somewhere."

Homer shrugged and raised his hands. "I thought you might be my dad."

"I thought you were allowed to stay here," I countered. "If that's the case, why did you care if it was your dad or not?"

He seemed to instantly sober as his shoulders sagged downward. "My dad and I aren't on great terms. But I know where he keeps the key, so I crash here when I need somewhere to lie low."

My locked elbows loosened slightly. "Did you leave the shoe in the guest bedroom?"

His face seemed to pale, though it was hard to say for sure in the darkness. I sensed the energy and hope drain from him with every new fact that came to light.

"Maybe," he muttered.

"That shoe belongs to a missing girl," I told him, elbows locking again. "Where did you get it?"

Could Homer have something to do with Vivian's abduction? If so, this whole mystery had just become more convoluted, especially since he would have needed to know ahead of time that *Looking for Love* would be filming here and that those ladies would be on the beach. That's what I kept coming back to over and over again.

"It was in my dad's boat." Homer shrugged and let out a lip-flapping sigh. "That's all I know."

"Who did you let use your father's boat?" Riley asked.

"How'd you know I let someone use it?" Homer sounded dumbfounded.

"Lucky guess," Riley said. "So who used it? Or were you behind the abduction of an innocent woman?"

Homer's eyes widened, and he took a step back. Thankfully, there was nothing else there for him to knock over. "The abduction of an innocent woman? Whoa. I don't know what you're talking about."

"Then you better start talking." I raised my gun higher.

"Slow down! I promise—I don't know their names.

I was up at a bar in Clearwater bragging about the house and the boat." He shrugged again. "I was trying to impress the ladies. You know how that can be. Anyway, some guys there overheard me and cornered me outside when I tried to leave. They roughed me up until I gave them the key to the boat."

"You just handed the keys over? You just happened to have the keys with you, for that matter?" I questioned. "That seems like too much of a coincidence."

"I'm in between homes right now, so sometimes I sleep on the boat. Plus, I may or may not have been dangling the keys in front of the women when I was bragging."

Joey had said the boat pulled up to the shore on the night Vivian was abducted. The water wasn't that deep out there, not enough for a large boat to come ashore without hitting the bottom. "I thought your dad's boat was small."

Homer shrugged. "A place to sleep is a place to sleep. People don't bother me out there on the water."

"What happened next?" Riley asked.

"I went down to the marina the next day, and, to my surprise, the boat was there—with the keys even." Homer ran a hand over his face. "But there was also blood."

"What do you mean, there was blood?" I asked. That was one fact I hadn't heard yet. That was one fact Old Yeller hadn't mentioned.

"It was on the side of the boat, like maybe

someone had fallen overboard and hit their head on the way down. I don't know. But I didn't like it. I panicked. I hopped on board and rode it over to Caladesi with the intention of cleaning it up. But then I saw the police, so I ditched it and caught a ride on the ferry back to the shore. I saw the shoe on the boat and grabbed it before running."

"Why would you do that?" I asked, trying to keep the irritation out of my voice.

"Cause I don't want to go to jail, and it seemed like easy evidence to get rid of."

"But there were two sandals," I said. "Why did you leave one?"

He shrugged again. "I didn't see the other one. I wasn't sticking around long enough to look either."

"Why come back here?" I questioned, trying to put everything together. I had a feeling Homer had been acting while in a drug and alcohol induced haze, which meant that all of his actions didn't necessarily have to be logical to the common person. Drugs and alcohol could seriously limit the good decisions people made. Add stress and panic to that, and it was the recipe for disaster.

"I wasn't . . . what's the word?" he said.

"Thinking?" I filled in.

"Yeah, that's it." He snapped his fingers. "I wasn't thinking clearly. I came back here to leave the keys. That way if my dad asked if I had anything to do with this, I could tell him no. I was going to take the shoe with me and throw it into the ocean, but then I heard you guys downstairs. I dropped it and ran."

"Your were wearing a mask, though," Riley said.

He shrugged in a "duh" like motion. "I didn't want anyone to see me. Of course."

I was done questioning his logic—he had none. Instead, I moved to my next inquiry. "Tell us about the men who took your keys."

He looked beyond me a moment, as if trying to recall anything about them. "They reminded me of spoiled frat boys, you know? They acted like they had money. They were wearing fancy clothes and jewelry and carrying big guns."

It sounded like the guys who'd cruised into town a few days ago and tried to rent a boat from Larry's friend. Had they given up on doing that and decided simply to use other people's boats without their permission in the meantime?

Homer looked back and forth from Riley to me. "What are you going to do? Shoot me?"

"Shoot you?" I squealed. "Not unless you do something stupid. I mean, stupider than you've already done. But I have to call the police, Homer. A woman's life is on the line here. You have to tell them what you just told us."

He frowned. "Fine. But please don't tell my dad."

***

I almost hated to see the police and Homer leave because I knew that meant that Riley and I might launch into the first fight of our married life together.

I dreaded that.

I dreaded disappointing him—mostly just because I loved him so much that I wanted to see him happy.

Riley's arms were crossed as he turned toward me. We stood in the living room, and the dark windows beside us promised doom and gloom as they stared back at us like a black abyss.

"Why'd you come downstairs without me?" Riley said.

I nibbled on my bottom lip, wishing I could rewind things. Instead, I backed up, my shoulder hitting a floor lamp and sending pain over my skin. "I just thought I'd check things out."

"You could have gotten killed."

"If you had gone down, you could have gotten killed."

"Gabby . . ." He let out an exasperated sigh.

I raised my hands. "I know, I know. Look, I really am sorry. But I'm used to doing things on my own. This is going to take some adjustment. And just because we're married, I don't want you to think that you always have to be my protector. I like to stand on my own two feet."

"This isn't about that. I just need to know you're going to be safe."

"Riley, I wish I could know that. None of us knows that, though."

He reached for my waist but stopped halfway and dropped his hands. "I do know that. But I want to take care of you."

"And I love that about you. I should have woken you so we could have figured something out instead of simply *me* figuring something out. I will try to do better. I promise. Forgive me?"

"Of course, I forgive you."

Relief washed through me. "Good. Because I thought for sure I'd just ruined our honeymoon. Again."

I was sensing a theme here.

"You could never disappoint me, Gabby."

As much as I loved what he said, that was a pretty big expectation to fulfill. I could think of plenty of ways I might disappoint him. I hoped none of them came to fruition.

I glanced outside at the beach for a moment. The moon lit the sky and reflected on the water, showering the area with soft light.

Something on the beach caught my eye, and I moved closer to the window.

"What is it?" Riley asked.

"Riley, there's someone out there. On the beach."

He turned toward me. "What are we waiting for? Let's go check it out."

CHAPTER 8

So, even though it was four a.m., Riley and I found ourselves taking a romantic nighttime walk on the beach.

Okay, not really.

I mean, we *were* walking on the beach, and it *was* nighttime, and I suppose the atmosphere *kind of* made it romantic.

But we were actually doing something that thrilled me even more: we were following a lead.

In the distance, I could see the figure I'd spotted from inside the beach house. He stood on the shore, staring at the *Looking for Love* mansion. If he noticed we were coming, he didn't try to run away or even flinch for that matter.

Riley and I glanced at each other, slowing our steps for a moment.

Who was that? What was he doing? And what exactly would end up playing out over the next several minutes?

The questions rushed through my mind in an

instant. But I wasn't turning back now.

"It's Vince Daley, the guy who was supposed to be Mr. Eligible," Riley whispered.

"What's he doing out here?"

"Let's find out."

I reached for the gun I'd shoved into my waistband, just in case things turned ugly. A girl could never be too certain.

"Vince Daley?" Riley called.

The man turned toward us, and I feared he might run. His body seemed to stiffen with anticipation.

To my surprise, he remained still. "Yes?"

"I thought I recognized you," Riley said. "You were on *Looking for Love* last season."

"That's right."

As we got closer, I noted that Vince's muscles looked tight, his eyes shifty and uncertain, and his arms frozen. What was he up to out here?

"I really thought you were going to be the next Mr. Eligible," Riley continued. "Instead they gave it to Ricky. What were they thinking?"

It was a good thing he'd watched the show so he could make this sound believable.

Or Riley might actually believe this, which I found both adorable and disturbing. I'd stick with adorable. It was adorable.

Vince let out a bitter chuckle. "Yeah, tell me about it. Everyone knows Ricky isn't looking for love. He's looking for a good time. I guess producers are okay with that."

"You mean, producers like Wally?" I asked.

He scowled. "Nah, Wally seems like a good guy. It's Alastair. He's a money-hungry, soulless excuse for a man. He'll do anything to make a dime."

"Even stage having one of the contestants abducted?" I asked.

He jerked his gaze toward me. "You mean Vivian?"

"Yes, Vivian," I said softly.

"I wouldn't put it past him. That's why I'm out here now. I don't trust these guys."

I noticed the way his eyes filled with emotion and his jaw flexed. There was some deep emotion behind his words. "You cared about Vivian, didn't you?"

He remained silent a moment and continued to stare. "We met at a party before the show started and really hit it off, but she was already contracted to come on the show. We agreed if things didn't work out between her and Ricky that we'd talk again when all of this was over."

"You're the one she was talking to right before the show started airing," I muttered, putting it together with what Joey had told me.

He nodded. "That was me."

"What did you mean earlier when you said 'you wouldn't put it past Alastair'?" Riley asked.

"I think Alastair is up to something. I'm waiting to see what. When he messes up, I'm going to be there to catch him and shut down this whole operation."

"Why do you think you're going to see something

out here now?" Riley asked. "It's the middle of the night."

"I heard some men in the diner talking about how they've seen some suspicious boat activity out here at night. I want to see what's going on."

Before we could talk any more, a scream sounded in the distance.

We all took off running.

***

My lungs were burning by the time I reached the other side of the beach near the mansion. The sand slowed my steps considerably, but I was determined not to let the guys get too far ahead of me. By the time we reached the shore, I spotted Joey hunched on the sand, staring toward the water. Her shoulders were stooped, her arms drawn across her chest, and tears flowed down her cheeks.

Alastair raced from the house, as well as Wally and a few other people I didn't recognize. They all gathered around Joey.

So did a camera crew.

Riley and I knelt by Joey, as did Wally.

"Are you okay?" I asked.

She nodded, even though she looked anything but okay.

"Vince?" Alastair blurted, jerking his gaze away from Joey. "What are you doing here?"

Vince ignored him, his gaze going to Joey. "What happened?"

"I got a message from Alastair saying I should meet him out here," Joey said. "But when I got here, these men tried to snatch me. They must have been waiting behind those rocks on the jetty."

Everyone turned to Alastair. He raised his hands. "I didn't send any messages."

"Your name showed up on my phone," Joey said.

"You're not even supposed to have a phone," Wally added.

"Someone else must have sent it. I don't make it a habit to meet my contestants at night. It's a lawsuit waiting to happen."

I turned back to Joey, figuring I'd mull over Alastair's role in all of this later. "What happened next?"

"I screamed, everyone showed up, and the men went running," Joey said.

"How many of them were there?" I continued.

"Three. All wearing masks again." She shivered. "What am I going to do? Someone is determined to kill me."

"Why don't you release the poor girl from her contract and let her go home?" I asked Alastair.

"Who are you?" He cocked one eyebrow and stared at me like I was an operative from another network.

"I'm . . . I'm the girl next door."

"The girl next door?" His features perked with interest. "I had a series called that about ten years ago. It was about these girls who lived—"

"I'm not really interested in any of your shows," I

interrupted. "I just want to know what's going on here."

"We wish we knew also," Wally said. "We've hired the best to get to the bottom of this."

"You mean Elite?" I wanted to snort. I hated to admit it, but I had a bit of an edge to my voice. I didn't realize it until this very moment, but those guys rubbed me the wrong way. PI work was anything but the glamorous job they made it out to be.

"Yes, Elite."

"I heard those guys are just trying to get their own reality show," Vince said. "No substance, all flash."

"Where is this Elite team when you need them?" Riley asked.

"They're staying at a house down the street," Alastair said. "We didn't think the other girls were in danger. We had no reason to. The police indicated that this was an individual crime, not some kind of vengeance against the show."

Vince snorted. "You've made plenty of people mad and given them motive."

Alastair turned to him, fire flashing in his eyes. "How do we know you're not behind this?"

"We were talking to him when everything went down," Riley said. "I can vouch for his whereabouts."

"He has friends," Alastair muttered. "I think he was standing over there just watching everything go down like the Godfather or something. Narcissists. Everyone who's ever been on this show turns into one."

"You knew I should have been Mr. Eligible," he

growled. "But I wouldn't go this far. In fact, I think you're the one who staged all of this for ratings. I've noticed that your viewership is up by about 50 percent since all of this happened. I heard from inside sources that the network was going to pull the plug on the show if you didn't kill it this season."

I turned to him again. "Is that true?"

"Again, who are you?" Alastair asked. "Besides the girl next door."

"She's a forensic scientist," Riley said. "I wouldn't ignore her theories."

That seemed to make Alastair think twice. He shoved his shoulders back and stared at me for a moment.

"Ratings *have* sunk in recent seasons. It's not our fault that no one has actually gotten married after meeting on our show and that our audience is losing faith in this process. But I would never take things that far."

Wally, who'd stepped away from the crowd, hung up his cell phone and joined our conversation again. "I called the police. They're on their way."

"Joey, could I have a word with you?" I asked.

She stared at me a moment before nodding. "Sure."

We walked away from the crowd. I didn't want to do this here and now, but there was no other time. I had pressing questions, and, once the police arrived, I'd most likely be silenced.

I wasn't officially investigating this, but I'd been pulled into the thick of things enough times that I deserved some answers.

"Joey, there's something I can't figure out," I started.

I stared at the woman a moment. She was wearing another dress, this time a short blue number with strappy sandals. Mascara ran down her cheeks, and her hair had been tousled by the wind. She was definitely shaken.

She sniffled. "You can't figure out something? What's that?"

"No one knew you and Vivian were going to go for a walk that night. No one except you and Vivian. That means that whoever snatched Vivian somehow was privy to that information."

Her face seemed to pale enough to match the full moon overhead. "What's that mean?"

"Who knew you were meeting, Joey?"

"No one." She shook her head a little too adamantly.

"Did anyone overhear you?"

She remained quiet a moment. "No. I mean, I don't think so. I'm still not following, though. What are you saying, exactly?"

I shifted, hating to say what I was going to say next, but I knew I'd have to say it anyway. "Joey, is there any chance that those guys who snatched Vivian grabbed the wrong girl?"

"What?" She gasped, her hand going over her O-shaped lips.

"In the dark, you and Vivian would have looked a

lot alike—but what if they grabbed the wrong person? In order to remedy this mistake, someone lured you out here tonight to finish the job. Maybe you were the intended victim all along."

"Why would anyone want to snatch me?" Her hand traveled from her mouth to her heart.

"You tell me. Can you think of any reason?"

"N—n . . . no. Of course not. No." She denied it a little too adamantly.

She was hiding something, I realized. But I had no idea what.

"You also said, on that night Vivian was abducted, something about the men 'doing their jobs' and leaving. Why the odd choice of words?"

She shrugged. "It's just an expression."

"Is it?"

"Oh, look." She nodded in the distance. "The police are here. I've got to run."

Before I could ask any more questions, she ran toward the approaching officers, sand flying behind her. She may have been running toward the police, but in another way she was fleeing from something else, something I'd only scratched the surface of.

What was I missing here?

CHAPTER 9

"So, what are you thinking?" Riley asked as we sat across from each other at the breakfast nook.

Behind him, colors of the morning that had earlier smeared the sky into lovely shades of pink and gray began to fade as the day drew on. I was on my third cup of coffee, and my thoughts buzzed along with the caffeine shooting through my blood.

"We can essentially rule out Homer," I started, taking a sip of my coffee. As I moved my arms and my shirt scraped across my skin, I cringed. Seriously? When would this sunburn get better? "He was in police custody when this happened."

"Correct."

"Vince was with us, although I suppose he could be working with someone. I still don't know what his motive would be, unless he wants to ruin the show so badly that he'd do all of this. It would be extreme, but I have seen extreme before." As I mulled that over, I picked at a cream cheese danish in front of me.

"Vince is a strange mix of concerned about Vivian and angry with the show," Riley said. "Could he and Vivian have been plotting something?"

"My gut tells me he's not involved," I said, picking off a piece of glaze. "Guts can be wrong, but I don't think we should focus on him."

"I agree. How about Alastair? Did he really send that message to Joey?"

"He has no way of proving he did or didn't. I mean, sure, the message was sent from his phone, but that doesn't mean he sent it. Did he take it this far for ratings? It's a possibility."

Riley let out a sigh and rubbed the side of his ceramic coffee mug. "He seems so adamant against lawsuits that I think he'd be more careful."

"If none of them are involved, then where does that leave us?" I asked.

Riley leaned back into the white upholstered chair. I could tell his thoughts were heavy as he tried to figure all of this out. I valued his opinion and gave him time to process what we knew.

"What were you talking to Joey about?" he finally asked.

"About the fact that either Joey or Vivian may know the person behind this. Since those two were the only ones who knew about their meeting, then it only makes sense that one of them accidentally tipped off the abductors. Otherwise, how would they have known where to be and when?"

Riley frowned. "Maybe it was random. Maybe these guys were just looking for a victim, and those two were in the wrong place at the wrong time."

"I suppose that could be true, but why? There are plenty of other beaches that would have their fair share of single, beautiful women walking around. This beach is mostly for retirees. People who are vacationing would be hit-or-miss, especially at this time of year."

"That's a good point. So you think that Vivian was purposefully targeted?"

"Or Joey. In the dark they would look alike." I kept going back to that. I couldn't help but think there could be something to that theory.

"That's true. They do have similar features."

I remembered my earlier conversation with Joey and her reaction to my questions. "I asked Joey about it, and she acted really weird, like she knows more than she's letting on. I wish I could figure out a way to get the truth out of her."

"Sounds like a lot of theories. Now we have to figure out how to get some answers. We only have four days left here. The sooner we get this done, the quicker we can enjoy ourselves."

***

After I took a nap, I had an idea. But first I had to do some research.

I hopped on a computer in the corner that Mr.

Murphy had given us permission to use and did an Internet search on Joey Hedges. The official show page had a glowing bio and lovely pictures of the Wisconsin girl. But I wanted to find the other blogs that liked to exploit the ugly side of contestants.

And there were plenty of them.

I found one particularly interesting. It was supposedly from someone "in the know" and who regularly hung around past contestants. However, this person remained anonymous.

Mr. In-the-Know claimed that Joey might have been from Wisconsin but, like most of the contestants on the show, she now lived in LA as she tried to make it big in show business. According to this guy, that was why most of the contestants went on the show—they hoped it might be a stepping stone to greater things.

Joey—a former teacher—was apparently working as a waitress now, and she'd had a small part in a made-for-TV movie. Old pictures showed her partying with another man.

I checked the date in the description of the social media photos. If that data was correct, she was dating someone else right up until two weeks before the show started filming.

I zoomed in on the pictures of her boyfriend. He looked like the kind of guy who liked to be on the party scene, with his expensive clothes, flashy jewelry, and a cocky expression. He also looked like the type who could be trouble. There was just something about the glint in his eyes that seemed to scream, "Don't mess with me."

"What did you find out?" Riley said, leaning in behind me.

Don't touch my shoulders. Don't touch my shoulders.

Thankfully, he didn't.

"Not much," I told him. "But maybe a lot. I'm not sure yet. I just know I really need to talk with Joey. I can't help but think she has some answers."

"I can probably arrange that. You remember when she asked me to be her lawyer, and I hooked her up with my friend Devin? I could probably pull some strings for you and arrange a meeting."

I felt my eyes light with hope. "Would you?"

"Anything for you."

"You're the best."

He smiled down at me. "You mean that?"

"Always and forever."

***

We were able to meet with Devin and Joey two hours later at the *Looking for Love* estate. Alastair escorted us— including Devin—into a private room away from cameras and any nonessential personnel.

I'd been fascinated on the way through the house. Little confessional booths had been set up in a couple of the rooms, and women cried in those corners as they talked about how much they loved Ricky. A cameraman

filmed it all. Wine glasses and bottles were everywhere—
and I did mean everywhere. Even the bathroom. I
supposed the producers counted on the fact that alcohol
brought out a more interesting side of their contestants—
which made for better TV.

The rest of the women had gone outside for a pool
party. Elite was wandering around the premises, but I felt
like they were flirting with the ladies more than acting as
PIs or bodyguards. Wally schmoozed with Ricky, as well as
the ladies.

As I sat on a plush couch beside Riley, I observed
Joey a moment. She still looked scared. Her eyes were
wide, her chin trembled every so often, and her arms were
drawn across her chest.

"Thanks for meeting with us," I told her. "I know
you're wondering why I asked you to meet with us here."

She nervously twisted her fingers together. "To say
the least."

"I have some experience in solving crimes," I said.
"And I want to help you."

"I need all the help I can get."

"I wanted to come to you first before the police."

Her eyes widened. "The police?"

I nodded. "Things aren't adding up, Joey."

"Like . . . like what? What do you mean?"

I leaned toward her, wondering just how
professional I looked with a raccoon face. "I need you to
be honest with me. I feel like there's more to your story,
that there's something you're not telling us. Did you know

the men who abducted Vivian?"

She let out a sob and stared at her hands. "I don't know. Maybe. Maybe not. I wish I could be sure."

"What do you mean?" I asked, more curious than ever.

"Before I came on the show, I was in a relationship with this awful man. His name is Skip. He was a drug dealer and so controlling. He always said if I left him, he'd kill me. I didn't really think a lot of it—until I met a woman while partying one night. She told me her best friend had once dated Skip and that she'd gone missing a year ago. No one had seen or heard from her since then. It really shook me up. I thought: that could be me. I knew I had to get away or I'd end up dead."

"What did you do?" I asked.

"A friend of mine who's an actress told me they were looking for some women for this show. I applied and was accepted," she said. "It seemed like the perfect escape. It just so happened that Skip was out of town when everything was set into motion, so the timing was ideal, to say the least. I packed my things, and I left for the show. I didn't look back. I knew he'd never be able to find me."

She frowned.

"What?" I questioned.

She squeezed her lips together. "I got word right before we left for Florida that my friend had died. It was supposedly in a waterskiing accident, but I know her. It was no accident."

"You think Skip was behind it?" Riley asked.

She nodded. "I know he was."

"And now you suspect that he's found you here?" I clarified.

She sniffled again. "I have no idea. I just know I've been in fear for my life. I've been afraid from the start that Skip was behind all of this."

"Why would he want to kill you?" I asked. I mean, controlling, abusive men didn't need a reason. But I wanted to hear her thoughts.

"I know too much." Her hands trembled now. "Skip . . . he's not a good guy. He's into drugs. More than into them. He deals them. I know about his operations, and I could bring him down. He's not going to let me do that."

Someone who was a drug dealer would have the resources to be able to carry out an abduction like the one Vivian had been through.

Now that we knew the who and why, we had to figure out where Skip and his minions might be now.

We also needed to find out how he'd discovered where Joey was hiding. He'd grabbed Vivian before the first episode even aired. Of course, he could have gotten information from Joey's friend—the woman who told Joey they were looking for contestants for the show. She had ended up dead.

Men with money and resources were looking for Joey and determined to silence her.

Four men.

Slick.

Partiers.

Could it be Elite? They had rolled into town awfully fast. They'd appeared on the beach that day to question Riley and me, which would have been the perfect guise for finding out how much we knew.

The question pressed on my mind. I just might be onto something. The theory was worth exploring.

I stepped from the room and found Alastair in the kitchen talking to Wally. "Could I have a moment?" I asked.

"Sure thing." He walked toward the counter to meet me.

I could tell by the way he studied my face that he thought my sunburn was just as obnoxious as it truly was. I was never going to live this down.

"What can I do for you?" he asked.

"I'm curious: How did you hear about Elite Security?"

He stared at me, his eyes beady-looking and calculating. "Through another producer. Why?"

I ignored his question. "Where are the men from Elite staying?"

He offered a quick, jerky shrug. "Why do you want to know that?"

"I'll explain in a moment. I can only assume they're not staying here at the mansion."

"Here?" He laughed. "No way. These women would go crazy over them. They're staying in a house on the other side of the island. Why?"

I remembered when we'd followed those guys in the boat yesterday. They'd disappeared on the bay side of the island . . . just like where Elite was staying.

What if the men who were supposed to be the good guys were actually the bad guys? The number of men in the organization matched the number of men behind Vivian's abduction. They also matched their description. Joey had even said they were "militant," and I knew Elite hired ex-cops and military.

"You think Elite are the ones who snatched Vivian?" Wally's voice was tinged with disbelief.

I'd been looked at like I was crazy many, many times before. I couldn't care less what they thought about me. I only wanted to get some answers.

I shoved my hip against the counter, trying to choose my words carefully. "They fit the description of the men who are involved in this. Plus, they were unaccounted for during the latest abduction attempt. And I think whoever is behind this has an inside connection with the show."

"Why would you think that?" Alastair splayed his hands on the marble countertop as he stared at me like a pit bull about to attack.

If he thought he was going to intimidate me with that stance, he was wrong. I'd faced giants before, and I had no plans of backing down now.

Copying him, I splayed my hands on the counter and stared back at him. "Because whoever is behind this knows too much about the operations of your show.

Because someone was close enough to you to grab your phone and send a text message. Who gave Joey her phone anyway?"

Alastair frowned and backed off, crossing his arms. I'd gotten through to him, I realized. I made him see my perspective. That was half the battle sometimes.

"I did," Alastair said. "I gave Joey her phone back, though it's supposed to be against the rules. I thought it might make her feel safer about her stay here."

"Did you send that text message?" I asked.

He gawked. "No. Of course not. I don't know why my name popped up on her screen."

I stepped back and set my jaw. I knew what I had to do, and I had to do it now before anyone else got hurt.

"I've got to call Chief Yeller and tell him my theory," I announced. "The bad guys could have been right under your nose this whole time."

***

Word spread quickly around town and around the cast and crew of *Looking for Love* about what was happening. The police were currently searching the rental home where Elite Security was staying. The guys had willingly let them inside, but each of them sent death looks at Riley and me as we stood on the lawn outside their place.

We weren't the only ones there. Alastair had also come, and several locals joined the crowd.

Could this be where Vivian was being held? Was

Elite behind this the whole time? And what did all of this have to do with Joey, if anything? Perhaps Skip had hired Elite to nab Joey after she'd escaped him. Only Elite had grabbed the wrong person.

The pieces were on the verge of fitting together, but they weren't quite there yet.

"What do you think they'll find?" Riley whispered. He stood beside me with his arms crossed. A brisk wind swept over the landscape, bringing with it tiny pieces of sand that irritated my skin in perfect harmony with my sunburn.

I saw some storm clouds in the distance and realized that rain was on its way. That would be sure to clear out the unwanted gawkers here. Of course, I supposed that included Riley and me.

"I'm not sure," I finally told Riley. "I hope it's Vivian. Although, I keep thinking about that blood that Homer told us he found on the side of the boat. I hope that doesn't mean she's hurt . . . or worse."

"I agree."

I stared at the house again. It was large, white, and covered in shingles. It had the same charm as the rest of the houses in the area, with its massive size yet cozy beach feel. Two Jeeps were parked out front, and I noted some beer cans in the flowerbeds.

Elite had been partying while they were here. It seemed like a lot of people did that. But a respectable PI firm should stay sober while on the job. In my book they should, at least.

"When we were out on the boat yesterday with Larry, we followed the men in that other boat, and they disappeared somewhere around this side of the island," I whispered to Riley. "It could have been here."

"I suppose it's a possibility. There is a boathouse in the back."

Chief Yeller exited the house at that moment and motioned to his officers and then to the men from Elite. They immediately pulled out handcuffs and arrested the PIs.

I sucked in a quick breath. What exactly had they found inside? Obviously, not Vivian because she was nowhere to be seen.

Oh no—please tell me they didn't find Vivian's dead body. Please.

I kept watching, waiting for a sign of what had happened. I held my breath. Prayed.

Yeller sauntered up to us a few minutes later, after the Elite guys were placed in the back of two police cruisers. "Good work, Mr. and Mrs. Thomas. We found a ransom video on one of the computers inside. Vivian was on it. We're taking them in, hoping with the right pressure they'll tell us where Vivian is."

"Really?" I asked.

I didn't know why the question slipped out. I guess, in part, that seemed too easy. I'd expected more of a search, of a struggle.

"Really. My men are going to stay here and look for more evidence. We'll keep you abreast."

Alastair was on the phone in the distance. He paced, looking furious that someone he'd hired was involved. A camera crew in the background filmed it.

Maybe he wasn't *that* furious, after all. Maybe this was all for show. I could never tell around these guys.

"Your hunch was right," Riley said. "Maybe we'll have some answers soon."

"We can only hope." There was still one thing that bothered me. These men weren't here on the first night when Vivian was abducted. How did they know the ladies were going outside?

Just then, Wally sidled up beside us. His face looked drawn and tight. Maybe everything was starting to get to him. After all, he was the one who always had to put on a cheery face, not only for the cast in the house but also for the viewers at home.

He leaned closer. "There's something I think you need to know," he whispered. "It's about Alastair."

I glanced at Riley before asking, "What?"

He scanned the crowds. "I can't tell you here. Follow me."

My blood spiked. Had he found something? Did he know something that we didn't?

We followed him across the yard, away from any listening ears. The clouds were over us now, making the atmosphere feel ominous. It was already late—nearly seven. Darkness would be falling soon.

As we rounded the side of the house, just out of sight, Wally turned. He had a gun in his hand. Pointed at us.

He was a part of this? He'd been the inside source this whole time, hadn't he?

"I'm sorry, guys," he muttered, sweat scattered across his forehead. "You were never supposed to get involved in this, though."

CHAPTER 10

"Wally, you don't have to do this," I told him.

"I wish I didn't. But I do." He wiped his forehead and gulped in shallow breaths.

"We can just walk away right now and pretend none of this happened," I told him.

The gun trembled in his hands. "I can't walk away. Can't you see?"

"Why are you doing this?" Riley nudged me behind him just as a big, fat drop of rain landed on my arm.

Thunder rumbled overhead as if God himself was warning us of bad things to come.

"We don't have time to talk. I need you to get in the boat. It's in the boathouse. No one will see us. We can finish this there."

"But—" I started.

He raised his gun higher. "No buts. We don't have time for this. You need to move."

"What are you going to do with us?" I asked as we walked toward the bay, our hands raised in the air.

"That remains to be seen." He wiped his forehead again. "I'm hoping it looks like you two were swept out to sea."

He was nervous. Like, really, really nervous. But why?

"There's a storm coming," Riley said. "You don't want to be out on the water."

"That's why I'm not going to be. You both will be, though. Now move." I felt something jam into my back. The gun.

We had no choice but to continue walking. As we did, I glanced over at the house next door. No one could see us. The house was angled in just the right way to conceal us.

What were we going to do?

"Please, Wally. Can't we just work this through?" I said, afraid if we got in that boat that we'd never be seen again.

He didn't say anything for a moment and then shook his head frantically. "It's too late."

"It's never too late," Riley said.

"Look," he paused, his chest heaving. Not from exertion. We weren't walking that fast. So why was he so anxious? "I don't have a choice in this."

"What are you talking about?" I asked. His words caused me to pause. What did that mean?

"You're what's called collateral damage. I don't want to hurt you. I don't. But I've been ordered to get rid of you two. You're too much of a risk."

"Who ordered you to get rid of us?" I asked.

He glanced around. "It's a long story. Now into the boathouse. We don't have any time to waste."

As soon as we stepped into the boathouse, I knew I had my chance. I swung my leg, and it connected with Wally's gun. Wally was many things, but he wasn't a fighter. At least, that was what I was counting on.

The gun flew in the air and slid across the pier before finally plopping into the water below. Thank goodness. But this battle wasn't over yet.

Riley charged toward Wally, tackling him. They both flew into the wall. The whole building shook with the impact.

I held my breath as I watched, wanting to step in. But as arms and fists flew, I had no way of inserting myself. Not yet, at least.

Wally smashed his elbow back, hitting Riley in the stomach. Riley only hunched in pain for a moment before getting a second wind. He grabbed Wally, twisted him around, and put him in a headlock.

"Please. Stop. Please." Wally struggled for breath and clawed at Riley's arms. "They have my wife."

Riley's grip loosened. "What are you talking about? You have five seconds to explain."

"Please! Those men grabbed my wife. They said if I told anyone, that she'd die. I had to go along with their plan or they'd kill her. I don't mean you any harm. I promise I don't."

His words washed over me until my pulse pounded

in my ears. "It's Joey's ex-boyfriend, isn't it? He's behind all of this."

Wally's eyes widened. "How'd you know?"

"It's all starting to come together."

"Skip cornered me on my front lawn before we left for Florida and told me to hire Elite, probably to throw the authorities off his trail. He came to me last week when he discovered Joey was on the show. I guess as soon as her name popped up on the show's website, he panicked. He had some kind of alert system in place in case her name ever came up online."

"You overheard Joey and Vivian were going to meet?" I asked.

He nodded. "I did."

"What about that ransom video?"

"I planted it on their computer when I knew the guys from Elite were out."

"So Elite was a scapegoat this whole time," I muttered.

"I told Alastair my friend suggested them. Skip was pulling the strings, though. He knew they'd be perfect for framing."

"Where are these guys now, Wally?" Riley asked.

"I'm not sure. I just know they're going to grab Joey the first chance they can get. She knows too much, and Skip is afraid she'll spill the beans on his operation."

"We've got to find them before they get Joey," I muttered. "Now."

"What about me? My wife? Please. You can't just

let her die."

    I bit down hard. He was right. There was more than one life on the line here. This situation would have to be handled carefully.

***

Thirty minutes later, we had a plan. It may have been a stupid plan, but I hoped it would work because it was all we had.

    As darkness fell and the storm raged around us, Wally had sent a small rowboat out into the bay. The vessel was empty, but the men who had his wife wouldn't know that. Not yet, at least.

    Wally had taken a picture of Riley and me lying inside the boat, looking dead. He'd send that photo to Skip as proof that he'd finished us off. Skip would hopefully assume that our bodies were swept out to sea in the storm.

    Wally had also promised that he would go back to the house and look after Joey. He assured us he wouldn't let anything happen to her, which meant she couldn't be alone and she would never go out on the beach by herself. I hoped he was as good as his word because if Skip found her, I feared she would end up dead.

    Meanwhile, Riley and I had darted through yards and behind trees in an effort to disappear. And by disappear, I mean we'd gone to Larry's house. He'd told us where he lived while we were on the boat yesterday. It was a condominium near the causeway leading to the island.

By the time we got there, we were soaked. And cold. And sandy.

Thankfully, Larry had been awake when we got there, even though it was still dark outside. He'd agreed to go along with our plan, which involved him starting a rumor that our bodies had washed ashore in the wee hours of morning. All he had to do was start the gossip chain down at Erma's, and it would spread through the locals in town.

"You really think we can pull this off?" Riley asked as we sat on Larry's couch drinking some coffee as morning approached. Another night with no sleep had left us both exhausted and running on caffeine and adrenaline.

"I hope so. Let me see that picture one more time."

Riley pulled out his phone. Wally had forwarded us a text Skip had sent him. It was a photo of his wife, Cheryl, bound and gagged, with the message, "Do it or she dies" beneath it.

Chilling, really. Especially when I saw Cheryl's eyes, which looked big with fright in the shadowed picture. Her hands were bound to the arms of a wooden chair. The wall behind her was old, rough wood.

I stared at the picture, trying to ascertain any clues possible about it. The window in the background was my best hope.

"Can you blow the picture up a little more?" I asked Riley.

He stretched it larger, focusing in on the window. "Do you see something?"

"If you look at it, it almost appears that's the causeway in the background," I muttered. "It's faint, but it's there. What do you think?"

He studied it a moment. "You could be right. You think they have her here on Crystal Key?"

"It's a possibility worth examining. We never asked where she was snatched. Even if it wasn't Florida, maybe they hauled her here with them. Guys like that, they have resources. They could have chartered their own plane."

Just then, the front door opened, and Larry and Leonard stepped inside. They had two plates in hand.

"We told Erma this breakfast was for us," Leonard said. "We just wanted it to go. I hoped you didn't think we'd be cooking for you."

"Not at all," I told them.

Leonard plopped the food on the table in front of us. "Well, here you go. Eat up."

"You didn't have to do this," Riley said.

"Course we did," Larry said. "We start a rumor you've died and then you're found starved in this condo? I want to spend my last days fishing, not in some jail."

"I can't argue that," I said.

I pulled the foil back from the plate, and the scent of eggs, bacon, and homemade fries drifted up toward me. My stomach grumbled. I hadn't realized how hungry I was.

"How did the rumor starting go?" Riley asked.

Leonard nodded. "Not too bad. Everyone believes

it right now. It won't take long for people to start talking to Old Yeller, though. Then they'll know the truth."

"Guys, are there any secluded houses on this island?" I asked. "Any places that are off the beaten path, probably bayside?"

Larry thought about it a moment before nodding. "I suppose there are a couple of places that were purchased back before this was a retirement hotspot. I heard property used to be dirt cheap here back in the day. Anyway, there's supposedly an old fishing cabin out by the Preserve."

"Where's the Preserve?" I asked.

"Midway on the island, bayside," Larry said. "It's mostly mangrove and banyan trees. But if you turn down this shell-lined driveway and keep going, you'll eventually find what we call the Homestead."

"Does anyone live there?" Riley asked.

"I understand you can rent it," Leonard said. "Most people come here wanting luxurious. This place is anything but. Not normal for this community at all."

I turned to Riley. "We need to go there."

"It's a bit far to walk," Larry said.

"Walking could be a problem anyway because we're supposed to be dead," Riley said. "We can't exactly go get our car and drive there either."

"You can take my golf cart," Larry said.

"Your golf cart?" I repeated.

He nodded. "Put some Hawaiian shirts on. We'll give you a couple of fishing caps. Go fast enough and everyone in town will assume they're seeing me and Leonard."

"Are you sure?" I questioned.

Leonard nodded. "Mark our words."

***

We'd given strict instructions to Larry and Leonard that if we weren't back in an hour to call Old Yeller and explain to him what was going on. Perhaps we should have called the police chief first, but since investigating that house last night had been a false alarm, I figured we wanted to be certain before crying wolf.

I felt ridiculous in the oversized Hawaiian shirt that smelled like Brylcreem. I'd pulled my hair back into a fishing cap and donned some sunglasses. Riley had done the same—minus the hair. We were a sight.

At least the loose clothing didn't irritate my skin.

"You really think Cheryl and Vivian could be here?" Riley asked as we cruised down the road.

"We won't know unless we look." I pointed in the distance. "I think that's where we turn."

The directions had been sketchy. Go past a big blue house then follow the woods past two palm trees, and you'll find a small forest of banyan trees. Turn at the first driveway and travel until you reach the mangrove trees at the end.

Not only was I potentially finding a bad guy, but I was also getting a botany lesson in the process.

Riley slowed as we approached a small road that was hidden among the trees and other tropical vegetation I couldn't identify.

Leonard's final warning echoed in my head: Watch out for rattlesnakes.

Not comforting.

As we saw a clearing at the end of the road, we slowed. Riley slipped the golf cart between some trees, and we started the rest of the way on foot. There was no need to announce our arrival.

Finally, a small cabin came into sight. Larry and Leonard were right: the place was a dump compared to the rest of the homes on the island. Definitely one of the originals.

"This could be the spot," Riley muttered. "The wood on the outside walls looks the same as the photo of Cheryl, and even from here I can see the causeway in the background."

"There are no cars here right now. Let's peek inside."

We crept closer to the house, remaining low and quiet. Finally, once we reached the edge of the woods, we gave one last glance at the driveway. When we saw no one was coming, we darted toward the house and pressed ourselves against the grungy wood siding.

The crawlspace was propped up on cinder blocks, and numerous pieces of trash littered the ground beneath it. High grass shot up around the edges.

If there was ever a good place for a snake to hide,

this was it.

Riley glanced in the first window.

"What do you see?" I asked. The window was too high for me to get a good look.

"Nothing. Just an empty, dumpy living room. There are some chip bags and soda bottles that look fairly new."

"Let's keep looking. We don't have much time."

We hurried to the next window. An empty kitchen.

We skirted around the backside of the house, and, as I did so, I spotted a boathouse at the end of a bulkheaded pier.

Was this where the men had disappeared when we followed them that day on the water? It was a good possibility.

We darted to one of the windows on this side of the house. This would be a perfect spot for that picture to have been taken. It was facing the water.

I glanced back.

And I could see the causeway.

Riley boosted himself up to get a better look. "They're here, Gabby. Vivian and Cheryl. They're really here."

My adrenaline surged. "Are they okay?"

"They're tied up, but they're alive."

Just then, I heard a boat humming in the distance. The men were coming back.

"We've got to hide," I mumbled.

We darted back into the thick grove of creepy-looking banyan trees before we could be spotted.

"Let's call the chief," I told Riley. "We can't do this on our own. If these guys are as scary as Joey said, we shouldn't mess with them."

"I agree." Riley pulled out his phone and dialed.

As he did, the boat pulled into the decrepit boathouse. A few minutes later, three men got out.

I recognized one of them as Skip. I couldn't make out what they were saying. Hardly anything, at least.

I did hear, "Grab Joey, and get out of here." "Load up the boat." "Rest of the crew arriving soon."

Great. Time was working against us.

Even more-so than I'd assumed.

Five minutes after the men entered the house, they exited with Vivian and Cheryl in tow.

The good news was that the women were alive. We just had to keep it that way.

"Those two nosy neighbors are dead," Skip muttered. "Apparently their bodies washed up on shore this morning. Plus Wally sent me pictures."

"What are you doing with these two?"

"They know too much. We need to get rid of them."

"And Joey?"

"Her too. Her testimony at trial would put me away for life. I can't let that happen."

His words left a cold sense of urgency in my gut.

I needed to quickly come up with a plan to keep all of us from getting killed.

CHAPTER 11

"We need to stop them," Riley muttered as he crouched beside me.

I stared at the scene playing out in front of us. "I know. But we need to do it without getting ourselves killed. I mean, honeymoon tragedies are the worst. It's not the way I want to make it onto *Dateline*."

"Maybe we could just buy time until Old Yeller arrives," Riley said.

"What else can we do?"

My muscles tensed, ready to act. Before I could act, movement in the distance caught my eye.

Someone charged from the other side of the lawn.

My eyes widened when I saw who it was. Homer Murphy.

What was he doing here? Was he a part of this? If not, how had he found us? My gut told me he wasn't on their side.

"He's going to get himself killed," I whispered. I closed my eyes, praying for wisdom. And a good outcome. So many innocent lives were on the line.

Skip pulled out his gun and aimed it at Homer. The women screamed. Skip's minions jumped into action.

"The police are offering a reward for anyone with information on you," Homer yelled. "I need that money, so hand those ladies over."

This was just awesome. Homer was not only trying to be a hero, but he was high while doing so. He had no idea the consequences he might face.

I expected the men to shoot him on the spot. Instead, Skip started laughing. He thought this was hysterical, I realized.

"You think we're just going to hand them over?" Skip said. "In case you haven't noticed, you're outnumbered."

"I tracked you down after talking to some guys at the bar," Homer said. "I heard you've been taking people's boats on joyrides. It wasn't hard to find you here."

The good news was that Homer had bought us some time. Where was Yeller? This island wasn't that big. It shouldn't take him too long to get here.

Skip's minions shoved the women closer to the woods—closer to us. If we could just grab them . . .

"What do you want to do?" Riley whispered.

"We've got to get the women away from those guys, especially if they start firing." The problem was, how did we safely do that? I wasn't sure.

Homer stepped closer, all drunken courage and ignorance. "Hand them over." He held up his gun. "Now."

Skip laughed even harder. "You're crazy if you think

we're going to hand them over."

I reached into my purse and pulled out my own gun. I didn't want to use it. I *really* didn't want to use it. There was so much that could go wrong.

But if Skip got away with these women, they were going to die.

Which was the lesser of two evils?

I couldn't let the innocent suffer, I realized. I had to do something.

"We need to grab them while we can," I whispered. "They get on that boat and they're dead."

Just then, Homer charged toward Skip. The men fired. The women screamed.

Riley and I jumped into action.

We dove toward Vivian and Cheryl, desperate to keep them away from the gunfire. Riley threw Cheryl on the ground, covering her body with his. I grabbed Vivian, knocking her out of the line of fire. The pain that ripped across my skin on contact was the least of my worries at the moment.

Her eyes widened in fear when she saw me, but I didn't have time to explain other than muttering, "We're here to help."

Bullets continued to fly around us. Our arrival had offered a distraction, apparently. While Skip looked back to see what was going on, Homer managed to hit him in the arm with a bullet.

The man muttered in pain and clutched his bicep.

One of Skip's men fired back, and Homer fell to the

ground.

No!

That was when Skip turned his full attention on Riley and me. He still grasped his arm, where blood burst. But his adrenaline and vengeance must have kept him going.

"Well, well, well," he said. "I guess good old Wally didn't finish the two of you off after all. I'm going to have to have a long talk with him about that."

"Just let us go," I told him. "We don't want trouble."

"You couldn't prove that by me," Skip said. He reached for his gun, his face twisted with pain. Nothing was going to stop him. "Now we have four people to take care of. I should have just finished you all off myself and saved all of us a ton of trouble."

I hovered in front of Vivian, trying to shield her from this.

Just then, another gunshot rang out. I froze, fearing I'd been fired on.

Then I saw Skip sink to the ground.

My gaze jerked behind him. Homer. Homer wasn't dead. He'd found enough strength to pull the trigger one more time.

As Skip's men turned toward Homer, I kicked Skip's gun out of the way before grabbing my own.

Homer hit another of the men in the shoulder. The gun flew from his hand.

I aimed and shot the knee of another man.

Just as I did, police cars pulled down the road. Old Yeller was here.

Maybe all of this was really over.

CHAPTER 12

"Well, we have two more days here in Florida," Riley said as we lounged on the beach watching the sunset. "The bad guys are in jail. Your sunburn is healing nicely. We have no more excuses not to enjoy ourselves."

That was right. We'd found an all-natural sunburn solution of using vinegar and coconut oil. I'd slathered it all over me last night, and, to my surprise, my burn was considerably better this morning.

I leaned over and kissed him. "That's right. No more excuses."

"Though this wasn't the way I'd planned to spend our honeymoon, I'm glad we were able to help Vivian, Cheryl, and Joey," Riley said. "I wouldn't be able to live with myself if we'd sat back and done nothing."

"Just one more thing to love about you."

Commotion in the distance caught my eye. The cast of *Looking for Love* was packing up and getting ready to call it quits. With Wally being questioned as part of this investigation, Vivian having been kidnapped, and Elite having been framed, the whole season didn't stand a chance.

The good news was that Ricky had been offered a part in a movie, and Alastair was talking about using the women in a new series he was producing about life as modern singles. I had a feeling everything would work out.

Someone came running over to us across the sand. Joey.

She gave both Riley and me a hug. "I just wanted to say thank you. Without you both I might be dead right now. I can finally have my life back—a life without Skip. Devin thinks he'll be spending a long time in jail."

"One piece of advice," I started. "Stay away from guys like him. And Ricky."

"Of course. I'm not interested in dating anyone right now."

"Did Vivian ever tell you what she wanted to talk with you about?"

"Apparently Skip cornered her at the airport on our way here. We took two separate flights, so he didn't see me. He asked her if I was on the show. Anyway, she got weirded out, but for some reason she wanted to share that with me as a warning. Maybe she's not heartless after all."

Alastair lumbered through the sand to join us. "I wanted to add my thanks as well. We'll be airing two more episodes of the show. Ratings are through the roof, and we're hoping to start up next season early. If the two of you ever want to think about reality TV . . ."

"Definitely not interested," Riley said. "But thanks."

"Enjoy the rest of your vacation." Alastair waved before he and Joey walked away.

I drew in a long, contented breath.

Skip and his men were in jail. Homer had been scared straight and was now in rehab. The charges against Wally would probably be dropped, considering the circumstances. His wife was safe. Vivian was safe.

Meanwhile, Larry and Leonard were practically legends in town after people heard about their role in helping us put the bad guys away. Both of the men might as well have been Cary Grant the way all the single lady retirees looked at them now.

All in all, everything had worked out.

"I say we enjoy the beach, enjoy each other, and chill out," I finally said.

He grabbed my hand and squeezed. "I think that's a great idea."

"I love you, babe."

"I love you too."

"I feel like there's nothing I can't do with you by my side," I told him, meaning it with every ounce of my being.

"That's the highest compliment ever. Now, let's get to enjoying this honeymoon. You are wearing sunscreen, right?"

I touched my shoulder. "You know it."

"Just making sure."

I slid my sunglasses on before leaning toward him and planting another kiss on his lips. "We got swept away in this mystery. Now it's time to get swept away with each other."

###

If you enjoyed this book, you may also enjoy:

Squeaky Clean Mysteries

Hazardous Duty (Book 1)

On her way to completing a degree in forensic science, Gabby St. Claire drops out of school and starts her own crime-scene cleaning business. When a routine cleaning job uncovers a murder weapon the police overlooked, she realizes that the wrong person is in jail. But the owner of the weapon is a powerful foe . . . and willing to do anything to keep Gabby quiet. With the help of her new neighbor, Riley Thomas, a man whose life and faith fascinate her, Gabby seeks to find the killer before another murder occurs.

Suspicious Minds (Book 2)

In this smart and suspenseful sequel to *Hazardous Duty*, crime-scene cleaner Gabby St. Claire finds herself stuck doing mold remediation to pay the bills. Her first day on the job, she uncovers a surprise in the crawlspace of a dilapidated home: Elvis, dead as a doornail and still wearing his blue-suede shoes. How could she possibly keep her nose out of a case like this?

It Came Upon a Midnight Crime (Book 2.5, a Novella)

Someone is intent on destroying the true meaning of Christmas—at least, destroying anything that hints of it. All around crime-scene cleaner Gabby St. Claire's hometown, anything pointing to Jesus as "the reason for the season" is being sabotaged. The crimes become more twisted as dismembered body parts are found at the vandalisms. Someone is determined to destroy Christmas . . . but Gabby is just as determined to find the Grinch and let peace on earth and goodwill prevail.

Organized Grime (Book 3)
Gabby St. Claire knows her best friend, Sierra, isn't guilty of killing three people in what appears to be an eco-terrorist attack. But Sierra has disappeared, her only contact a frantic phone call to Gabby proclaiming she's being hunted. Gabby is determined to prove her friend is innocent and to keep Sierra alive. While trying to track down the real perpetrator, Gabby notices a disturbing trend at the crime scenes she's cleaning, one that ties random crimes together—and points to Sierra as the guilty party. Just what has her friend gotten herself involved in?

Dirty Deeds (Book 4)
"Promise me one thing. No snooping. Just for one week." Gabby St. Claire knows that her fiancé's request is a simple one she should be able to honor. After all, Riley's law school reunion and attorneys' conference at a posh resort is a chance for them to get away from the mysteries Gabby often finds herself involved in as a crime-scene cleaner. Then an old friend of Riley's goes missing. Gabby suspects one of Riley's buddies might be behind the disappearance. When the missing woman's mom asks Gabby for help, how can she say no?

The Scum of All Fears (Book 5)
Gabby St. Claire is back to crime-scene cleaning and needs help after a weekend killing spree fills her work docket. A serial killer her fiancé put behind bars has escaped. His last words to Riley were: *I'll get out, and I'll get even.* Pictures

of Gabby are found in the man's prison cell, messages are left for Gabby at crime scenes, someone keeps slipping in and out of her apartment, and her temporary assistant disappears. The search for answers becomes darker when Gabby realizes she's dealing with a criminal who is truly the scum of the earth. He will do anything to make Gabby's and Riley's lives a living nightmare.

To Love, Honor, and Perish (Book 6)
Just when Gabby St. Claire's life is on the right track, the unthinkable happens. Her fiancé, Riley Thomas, is shot and in life-threatening condition only a week before their wedding. Gabby is determined to figure out who pulled the trigger, even if investigating puts her own life at risk. As she digs deeper into the case, she discovers secrets better left alone. Doubts arise in her mind, and the one man with answers lies on death's doorstep. Then an old foe returns and tests everything Gabby is made of— physically, mentally, and spiritually. Will all she's worked for be destroyed?

Mucky Streak (Book 7)
Gabby St. Claire feels her life is smeared with the stain of tragedy. She takes a short-term gig as a private investigator—a cold case that's eluded detectives for ten years. The mass murder of a wealthy family seems impossible to solve, but Gabby brings more clues to light. Add to the mix a flirtatious client, travels to an exciting new city, and some quirky—albeit temporary—new sidekicks, and things get complicated. With every new development, Gabby prays that her "mucky streak" will end and the future will become clear. Yet every answer she uncovers leads her closer to danger—both for her life and for her heart.

Foul Play (Book 8)

Gabby St. Claire is crying "foul play" in every sense of the phrase. When the crime-scene cleaner agrees to go undercover at a local community theater, she discovers more than backstage bickering, atrocious acting, and rotten writing. The female lead is dead, and an old classmate who has staked everything on the musical production's success is about to go under. In her dual role of investigator and star of the show, Gabby finds the stakes rising faster than the opening-night curtain. She must face her past and make monumental decisions, not just about the play but also concerning her future relationships and career. Will Gabby find the killer before the curtain goes down—not only on the play, but also on life as she knows it?

Broom and Gloom (Book 9)

Gabby St. Claire is determined to get back in the saddle again. While in Oklahoma for a forensic conference, she meets her soon-to-be stepbrother, Trace Ryan, an up-and-coming country singer. A woman he was dating has disappeared, and he suspects a crazy fan may be behind it. Gabby agrees to investigate, as she tries to juggle her conference, navigate being alone in a new place, and locate a woman who may not want to be found. She discovers that sometimes taking life by the horns means staring danger in the face, no matter the consequences.

Dust and Obey (Book 10)

When Gabby St. Claire's ex-fiancé, Riley Thomas, asks for her help in investigating a possible murder at a couples retreat, she knows she should say no. She knows she should run far, far away from the danger of both being around Riley and the crime. But her nosy instincts and determination take precedence over her logic. Gabby and Riley must work together to find the killer. In the process, they have to confront demons from their past and deal with their present relationship.

Thrill Squeaker (Book 11)
An abandoned theme park. An unsolved murder. A decision that will change Gabby's life forever. Restoring an old amusement park and turning it into a destination resort seems like a fun idea for former crime-scene cleaner Gabby St. Claire. The side job gives her the chance to spend time with her friends, something she's missed since beginning a new career. The job turns out to be more than Gabby bargained for when she finds a dead body on her first day. Add to the mix legends of Bigfoot, creepy clowns, and ghostlike remnants of happier times at the park, and her stay begins to feel like a rollercoaster ride. Someone doesn't want the decrepit Mythical Falls to open again, but just how far is this person willing to go to ensure this venture fails? As the stakes rise and danger creeps closer, will Gabby be able to restore things in her own life that time has destroyed—including broken relationships? Or is her future closer to the fate of the doomed Mythical Falls?

Cunning Attractions (Book 12)
Coming soon

While You Were Sweeping, a Riley Thomas Novella
Riley Thomas is trying to come to terms with life after a traumatic brain injury turned his world upside down. Away from everything familiar—including his crime-scene-cleaning former fiancée and his career as a social-rights attorney—he's determined to prove himself and regain his old life. But when he claims he witnessed his neighbor

shoot and kill someone, everyone thinks he's crazy. When all evidence of the crime disappears, even Riley has to wonder if he's losing his mind.

Note: *While You Were Sweeping* is a spin-off mystery written in conjunction with the Squeaky Clean series featuring crime-scene cleaner Gabby St. Claire.

The Sierra Files

Pounced (Book 1)
Animal-rights activist Sierra Nakamura never expected to stumble upon the dead body of a coworker while filming a project nor get involved in the investigation. But when someone threatens to kill her cats unless she hands over the "information," she becomes more bristly than an angry feline. Making matters worse is the fact that her cats—and the investigation—are driving a wedge between her and her boyfriend, Chad. With every answer she uncovers, old hurts rise to the surface and test her beliefs. Saving her cats might mean ruining everything else in her life. In the fight for survival, one thing is certain: either pounce or be pounced.

Hunted (Book 2)
Who knew a stray dog could cause so much trouble? Newlywed animal-rights activist Sierra Nakamura Davis must face her worst nightmare: breaking the news she eloped with Chad to her ultra-opinionated tiger mom. Her perfectionist parents have planned a vow-renewal ceremony at Sierra's lush childhood home, but a neighborhood dog ruins the rehearsal dinner when it shows up toting what appears to be a fresh human bone. While dealing with the dog, a nosy neighbor, and an old flame turning up at the wrong times, Sierra hunts for answers. Her journey of discovery leads to more than just who committed the crime.

Pranced (Book 2.5, a Christmas novella)
Sierra Nakamura Davis thinks spending Christmas with her husband's relatives will be a real Yuletide treat. But when

the animal-rights activist learns his family has a reindeer farm, she begins to feel more like the Grinch. Even worse, when Sierra arrives, she discovers the reindeer are missing. Sierra fears the animals might be suffering a worse fate than being used for entertainment purposes. Can Sierra set aside her dogmatic opinions to help get the reindeer home in time for the holidays? Or will secrets tear the family apart and ruin Sierra's dream of the perfect Christmas?

Rattled (Book 3)
"What do you mean a thirteen-foot lavender albino ball python is missing?" Tough-as-nails Sierra Nakamura Davis isn't one to get flustered. But trying to balance being a wife and a new mom with her crusade to help animals is proving harder than she imagined. Add a missing python, a high maintenance intern, and a dead body to the mix, and Sierra becomes the definition of rattled. Can she balance it all—and solve a possible murder—without losing her mind?

Holly Anna Paladin Mysteries

Random Acts of Murder (Book 1)
When Holly Anna Paladin is given a year to live, she
embraces her final days doing what she loves most—
random acts of kindness. But one of her extreme good
deeds goes horribly wrong, implicating her in a string of
murders. Holly is suddenly thrust into a different kind of
fight for her life. Could it also be random that the
detective assigned to the case is her old high school crush
and present-day nemesis? Will Holly find the killer before
he ruins what is left of her life? Or will she spend her final
days alone and behind bars?

Random Acts of Deceit (Book 2)
"Break up with Chase Dexter, or I'll kill him." Holly Anna
Paladin never expected such a gut-wrenching ultimatum.
With home invasions, hidden cameras, and bomb threats,
Holly must make some serious choices. Whatever she
decides, the consequences will either break her heart or
break her soul. She tries to match wits with the Shadow
Man, but the more she fights, the deeper she's drawn into
the perilous situation. With her sister's wedding problems
and the riots in the city, Holly has nearly reached her
breaking point. She must stop this mystery man before
someone she loves dies. But the deceit is threatening to
pull her under . . . six feet under.

Random Acts of Murder (Book 3)
When Holly Anna Paladin's boyfriend, police detective
Chase Dexter, says he's leaving for two weeks and can't
give any details, she wants to trust him. But when she
discovers Chase may be involved in some unwise and

dangerous pursuits, she's compelled to intervene. Holly gets a run for her money as she's swept into the world of horseracing. The stakes turn deadly when a dead body surfaces and suspicion is cast on Chase. At every turn, more trouble emerges, making Holly question what she holds true about her relationship and her future. Just when she thinks she's on the homestretch, a dark horse arises. Holly might lose everything in a nail-biting fight to the finish.

Random Acts of Scrooge (Book 3.5)

Christmas is supposed to be the most wonderful time of the year, but a real-life Scrooge is threatening to ruin the season's good will. Holly Anna Paladin can't wait to celebrate Christmas with family and friends. She loves everything about the season—celebrating the birth of Jesus, singing carols, and baking Christmas treats, just to name a few. But when a local family needs help, how can she say no? Holly's community has come together to help raise funds to save the home of Greg and Babette Sullivan, but a Bah-Humburgler has snatched the canisters of cash. Holly and her boyfriend, police detective Chase Dexter, team up to catch the Christmas crook. Will they succeed in collecting enough cash to cover the Sullivans' overdue bills? Or will someone succeed in ruining Christmas for all those involved?

Random Acts of Greed (Book 4)

Coming soon

Carolina Moon Series

Home Before Dark (Book 1)

Nothing good ever happens after dark. Country singer Daleigh McDermott's father often repeated those words. Now, her father is dead. As she's about to flee back to Nashville, she finds his hidden journal with hints that his death was no accident. Mechanic Ryan Shields is the only one who seems to believe Daleigh. Her father trusted the man, but her attraction to Ryan scares her. She knows her life and career are back in Nashville and her time in the sleepy North Carolina town is only temporary. As Daleigh and Ryan work to unravel the mystery, it becomes obvious that someone wants them dead. They must rely on each other—and on God—if they hope to make it home before the darkness swallows them.

Gone By Dark (Book 2)

Charity White can't forget what happened ten years earlier when she and her best friend, Chloe, cut through the woods on their way home from school. A man abducted Chloe, who hasn't been seen since. Charity has tried to outrun the memories and guilt. What if they hadn't taken that shortcut? Why wasn't Charity kidnapped instead of Chloe? And why weren't the police able to track down the bad guy? When Charity receives a mysterious letter that promises answers, she returns to North Carolina in search of closure and the peace that has eluded her. With the help of her new neighbor, Police Officer Joshua Haven, Charity begins to track down mysterious clues. They soon discover that they must work together or both of them will be swallowed by the looming darkness.

Cape Thomas Mysteries:

Dubiosity (Book 1)
Savannah Harris vowed to leave behind her old life as an investigative reporter. But when two migrant workers go missing, her curiosity spikes. As more eerie incidents begin afflicting the area, each works to draw Savannah out of her seclusion and raise the stakes—for her and the surrounding community. Even as Savannah's new boarder, Clive Miller, makes her feel things she thought long forgotten, she suspects he's hiding something too, and he's not the only one. As secrets emerge and danger closes in, Savannah must choose between faith and uncertainty. One wrong decision might spell the end . . . not just for her but for everyone around her. Will she unravel the mystery in time, or will doubt get the best of her?

Disillusioned (Book 2)
Nikki Wright is desperate to help her brother, Bobby, who hasn't been the same since escaping from a detainment camp run by terrorists in Colombia. Rumor has it that he betrayed his navy brothers and conspired with those who held him hostage, and both the press and the military are hounding him for answers. All Nikki wants is to shield her brother so he has time to recover and heal. But soon they realize the paparazzi are the least of their worries. When a group of men try to abduct Nikki and her brother, Bobby insists that Kade Wheaton, another former SEAL, can keep them out of harm's way. But can Nikki trust Kade? After all, the man who broke her heart eight years ago is anything but safe... Hiding out in a farmhouse on the Chesapeake Bay, Nikki finds her loyalties—and the

remnants of her long-held faith—tested as she and Kade put aside their differences to keep Bobby's increasingly erratic behavior under wraps. But when Bobby disappears, Nikki will have to trust Kade completely if she wants to uncover the truth about a rumored conspiracy. Nikki's life—and the fate of the nation—depends on it.

Standalones:

The Good Girl
Tara Lancaster can sing "Amazing Grace" in three
harmonies, two languages, and interpret it for the hearing
impaired. She can list the Bible canon backward, forward,
and alphabetized. The only time she ever missed church
was when she had pneumonia and her mom made her
stay home. Then her life shatters and her reputation is left
in ruins. She flees halfway across the country to dog-sit,
but the quiet anonymity she needs isn't waiting at her
sister's house. Instead, she finds a knife with a threatening
message, a fame-hungry friend, a too-hunky neighbor, and
evidence of . . . a ghost? Following all the rules has gotten
her nowhere. And nothing she learned in Sunday School
can tell her where to go from there.

Death of the Couch Potato's Wife (Suburban Sleuth Mysteries)
You haven't seen desperate until you've met Laura Berry, a
career-oriented city slicker turned suburbanite housewife.
Well-trained in the big-city commandment, "mind your
own business," Laura is persuaded by her spunky seventy-
year-old neighbor, Babe, to check on another neighbor
who hasn't been seen in days. She finds Candace Flynn,
wife of the infamous "Couch King," dead, and at last has a
reason to get up in the morning. Someone is determined
to stop her from digging deeper into the death of her
neighbor, but Laura is just as determined to figure out who
is behind the death-by-poisoned-pork-rinds.

Imperfect
Since the death of her fiancé two years ago, novelist

Morgan Blake's life has been in a holding pattern. She has a major case of writer's block, and a book signing in the mountain town of Perfect sounds as perfect as its name. Her trip takes a wrong turn when she's involved in a hit-and-run: She hit a man, and he ran from the scene. Before fleeing, he mouthed the word "Help." First she must find him. In Perfect, she finds a small town that offers all she ever wanted. But is something sinister going on behind its cheery exterior? Was she invited as a guest of honor simply to do a book signing? Or was she lured to town for another purpose—a deadly purpose?

The Gabby St. Claire Diaries (a tween mystery series)

***The Curtain Call Caper* (Book 1)**
Is a ghost haunting the Oceanside Middle School auditorium? What else could explain the disasters surrounding the play—everything from missing scripts to a falling spotlight and damaged props? Seventh-grader Gabby St. Claire has dreamed about being part of her school's musical, but a series of unfortunate events threatens to shut down the production. While trying to uncover the culprit and save her fifteen minutes of fame, she also has to manage impossible teachers, cliques, her dysfunctional family, and a secret she can't tell even her best friend. Will Gabby figure out who or what is sabotaging the show . . . or will it be curtains for her and the rest of the cast?

***The Disappearing Dog Dilemma* (Book 2)**
Why are dogs disappearing around town? When two friends ask seventh-grader Gabby St. Claire for her help in finding their missing canines, Gabby decides to unleash her sleuthing skills to sniff out whoever is behind the act. But time management and relationships get tricky as worrisome weather, a part-time job, and a new crush interfere with Gabby's investigation. Will her determination crack the case? Or will shadowy villains, a penchant for overcommitting, and even her own heart put her in the doghouse?

***The Bungled Bike Burglaries* (Book 3)**
Stolen bikes and a long-forgotten time capsule leave one amateur sleuth baffled and busy. Seventh-grader Gabby

St. Claire is determined to bring a bike burglar to justice—
and not just because mean girl Donabell Bullock is strong-
arming her. But each new clue brings its own set of
trouble. As if that's not enough, Gabby finds evidence of a
decades-old murder within the contents of the time
capsule, but no one seems to take her seriously. As her
investigation heats up, will Gabby's knack for being in the
wrong place at the wrong time with the wrong people
crack the case? Or will it prove hazardous to her health?

Complete Book List

Squeaky Clean Mysteries:
#1 Hazardous Duty
#2 Suspicious Minds
#2.5 It Came Upon a Midnight Crime
#3 Organized Grime
#4 Dirty Deeds
#5 The Scum of All Fears
#6 To Love, Honor, and Perish
#7 Mucky Streak
#8 Foul Play
#9 Broom and Gloom
#10 Dust and Obey
#11 Thrill Squeaker
#11.5 Swept Away (a honeymoon novella)
#12 Cunning Attractions (coming soon)

Squeaky Clean Companion Novella:
While You Were Sweeping

The Sierra Files:
#1 Pounced
#2 Hunted
#2.5 Pranced (a Christmas novella)
#3 Rattled

The Gabby St. Claire Diaries (a Tween Mystery series):
#1 The Curtain Call Caper
#2 The Disappearing Dog Dilemma
#3 The Bungled Bike Burglaries

Holly Anna Paladin Mysteries:
#1 Random Acts of Murder
#2 Random Acts of Deceit
#3 Random Acts of Malice
#3.5 Random Acts of Scrooge
#4 Random Acts of Greed

Carolina Moon Series:
Home Before Dark
Gone By Dark
Wait Until Dark

Suburban Sleuth Mysteries:
#1 Death of the Couch Potato's Wife

Stand-alone Romantic-Suspense:
Keeping Guard
The Last Target
Race Against Time
Ricochet
Key Witness
Lifeline
High-Stakes Holiday Reunion
Desperate Measures
Hidden Agenda
Mountain Hideaway
Dark Harbor

Cape Thomas Mysteries:
Dubiosity
Disillusioned

Standalone Romantic Mystery:
The Good Girl

Suspense:
Imperfect

Nonfiction:
Changed: True Stories of Finding God through Christian Music
The Novel in Me: The Beginner's Guide to Writing and Publishing a Novel

About the Author:

USA Today has called Christy Barritt's books "scary, funny, passionate, and quirky."

Christy writes both mystery and romantic suspense novels that are clean with underlying messages of faith. Her books have won the Daphne du Maurier Award for Excellence in Suspense and Mystery, have been twice nominated for the Romantic Times Reviewers' Choice Award, and have finaled for both a Carol Award and Foreword Magazine's Book of the Year.

She is married to her Prince Charming, a man who thinks she's hilarious—but only when she's not trying to be. Christy is a self-proclaimed klutz, an avid music lover who's known for spontaneously bursting into song, and a road trip aficionado.
When she's not working or spending time with her family, she enjoys singing, playing the guitar, and exploring small, unsuspecting towns where people have no idea how accident-prone she is.

Find Christy online at:
www.christybarritt.com
www.facebook.com/christybarritt
www.twitter.com/cbarritt

If you enjoyed this book, please leave a review.

CHRISTY BARRITT

Made in the USA
Las Vegas, NV
23 March 2024

87675961R00094